Thomas Sedgwick Whalley

Edwy and Edilda

A tale - in five parts

Thomas Sedgwick Whalley

Edwy and Edilda
A tale - in five parts

ISBN/EAN: 9783337088347

Printed in Europe, USA, Canada, Australia, Japan

Cover: Foto ©Andreas Hilbeck / pixelio.de

More available books at **www.hansebooks.com**

EDWY and EDILDA,

A TALE,

IN FIVE PARTS.

BY THE

REV. THOMAS SEDGWICK WHALLEY,

AUTHOR OF

"A POEM ON MONT BLANC,"

&c. &c. &c.

EMBELLISHED WITH SIX FINE ENGRAVINGS,

FROM ORIGINAL DESIGNS,

BY A YOUNG LADY.

LONDON:

PRINTED FOR T. CHAPMAN, FLEET STREET; W. RICHARDSON, ROYAL
EXCHANGE; AND R. FAULDER, BOND STREET.

1794.

TO

LADY LANGHAM.

DEAR MADAM,

As the wishes of those I esteem and love
have the power of commands, this new Edi-
tion of the following Poem is published solely
at your desire.   I should have been delighted
to have rendered it, by any emendations, worthier of the Engravings which now embellish
it, from the hand of early genius, too early
chilled by the hand of death.   May the
Sisters in *merit* as well as *blood* of the
charming and amiable daughter you have so

long and fo deeply lamented, refemble her in
every thing but (what fond and fhort-fighted
mortals are too apt to call) an *untimely* fate!
Then they cannot fail to reflect back your
own virtues, and to prove the ornament of
your life, and the reward of all your tendernefs and cares.

You know how fincerely this, and every
good wifh towards you, flows from the heart
of

Your Ladyfhip's

Faithful and affectionate Friend and Servant,

May 1, 1794.

Thomas Sedgwick Whalley.

EDWY AND EDILDA:

A TALE.

———————

PART I.

WHEN *Egbert* England's fceptre fway'd,
   For pow'r and arms renown'd,
Brave *Galvan* liv'd; whofe deeds of youth
   By peaceful age were crown'd.

Full many a year his feet had trod
   The rougheft paths of war;
And in his mafter's caufe he earn'd
   Full many an honour'd fcar:

But deeds of hardiment at length
   Give place to filver hairs;
And feeble age, unlocking ftrength,
   His future fervice fpares.

Deep in the bofom of a vale,
   By Severn's rolling flood,
The hoary Warrior's native tow'rs
   With ample honours ftood.

B

Thither from camps and courts retir'd,
　The aged Baron fpent
His days, in long-forgotten peace,
　And long-unknown content!

His hofpitable hall was ftill
　With largeft bounty crown'd;
And many a health, and many a tale,
　His feftive board went round.

But ftill the healths to England's weal
　Moft copioufly flow'd;
And lengthen'd tales, of former wars,
　The patriot Warrior fhow'd.

And as the fame of *Egbert*'s arms,
　And tale of Britain's good,
Dwelt on the generous *Galvan*'s tongue,
　And warm'd his aged blood;

Unwonted flufhes o'er his face
　Would animating break;
And in his eyes unwonted fires
　The ardent heart would fpeak.

Nor did his cheek unufeful glow,
　Nor tongue defcant in vain;
Since lift'ning youth his ardour caught,
　And fired at his ftrain.

Thus *Galvan* liv'd, by grey hairs laid
　Upon the lap of eafe,
Honour and love, on every fide,
　Augmenting ftill his peace.

Nor thefe alone confpir'd to gild
　　The evening of his days ;
Nor did his heart alone dilate
　　With foreign love, and praife ;

A nearer, dearer, home-bred joy,
　　That heart more nearly charms ;
And in a darling Daughter's form,
　　His breaft more genial warms.

Of many children, fhe alone
　　To blefs his years remain'd ;
Who, from her mother long deceas'd,
　　Edilda had been nam'd.

Upon her cheek the virgin rofe
　　Had fpent its fofteft bloom ;
And from her coral lips did fhed
　　Its exquifite perfume.

Her hair in graceful ringlets flow'd,
　　Than filk more glofly far ;
And either beaming eye outfhone
　　The radiant morning ftar.

Yet fires through their fringes ftill
　　As foft, as piercing went ;
And every fparkling glance appear'd
　　With fweeteft languors blent.

Her fhape, her hair, her voice, her mien,
　　What eloquence can tell ?
What pen defcribe the countlefs charms
　　That round her lov'd to dwell ?

But not to outward charms alone
    Her merits were confin'd;
More weak were language to exprefs
    The beauties of her mind!

Within her foul each generous thought,
    Each noble tranfport glow'd;
And beaming from her fpeaking eye,
    To all confefs'd they ftood.

Yet ftill the foftnefs of her fex
    Moft ftrikingly prevail'd;
And from that foftnefs, fhe was firft
    The fweet *Edilda* hail'd!

Ah dangerous fweetnefs! which no force,
    No wifdom could withftand:
Ah dangerous foftnefs! that with love
    Would ftill go hand in hand.

For who that own'd a noble heart,
    Or could by charms be won,
But foon confefs'd *Edilda*'s pow'r,
    And bow'd before her throne?

Not *Galvan*'s worth, nor *Galvan*'s fway,
    Alone had fill'd his hall;
Far more the fweet *Edilda*'s charms,
    To glad obeifance, call.

And while the daughter's beauties bloom'd
    So lovely to the fight,
What wonder if the father's tale
    Afforded ftrange delight!

What wonder? where the purple blood
 In noontide currents flow'd,
And where defire of generous deeds
 In every bofom glow'd.

For every youth that lift'ning fat
 At *Galvan*'s plenteous board,
The goodly heir of noble blood,
 With lofty thoughts was ftor'd.

With lofty thoughts they all were ftor'd;
 But one of all around,
Without a claim to noble blood,
 Was unaffuming found:

Edwy the graceful youth was call'd;
 The ancient *Hilda*'s fon
By *Ongar*; who his mortal courfe
 Long fince in war had run.

An humble dwelling *Hilda* own'd;
 And but a fcanty flock;
Which *Edwy* us'd to watch all day,
 From off a neighb'ring rock:

There refting, with his pipe and book,
 Beneath a fpreading tree,
Full many a ditty he would play;
 And oft would poring be

Upon full many a copious tale
 Of war and warriors dread;
While winged hours unminded flew
 Above his youthful head:

A learned friar lov'd him well,
　For native wit and worth;
And to that learned friar, I ween,
　His knowledge ow'd its birth.

From him, or other wight, 't is plain
　His learning he muſt catch;
Since *Hilda*'s fortunes, but for this,
　Had plac'd it paſt his reach.

But that though now beyond our ken,
　Yet this is handed down;
That youthful *Edwy*, in thofe days,
　A fcholar rare was known.

A noted minſtrel too he was;
　And when his pipe did found,
The neighb'ring villages, to hear,
　Would quickly gather round:

The villagers would gather round,
　Till many a village fair,
Allur'd by *Edwy*'s pipe or face,
　Made *Edwy* all her care!

Yet, though compos'd of fofteſt mould
　His nature feem'd to be;
And open'd at the tender touch
　Of fenfibility;

To love's foft pains his gentle heart
　Averfe did ſtill appear;
Averfe, or cold, to all the charms
　Of ev'ry village fair!

For fomething in his manners mild
  Above his peers was feen ;
And in his foul a diff'rence yet
  Far greater was, I ween.

It happen'd on a fummer's morn,
  While on his fav'rite rock,
Beneath the beeches bow'ring fhade
  He fat, and watch'd his flock ;

That *Galvan*, fever'd from his train
  In hunting, carelefs ftray'd
Where *Edwy* on his mellow pipe
  Melodioufly play'd.

Charm'd with the fweet unwonted founds,
  That fudden caught his ear,
With cautious fteps behind the rock,
  He ftole, unfeen, to hear.

And while, with many a cadence clear,
  The youth purfu'd his ftrain ;
And many a wild note, foft and full,
  Refounded through the plain ;

Behold, a fierce and famifh'd wolf
  Rufh'd from a thicket by,
And on the hoary warrior's throat
  Flew, with a dreadful cry !

Unarm'd, unwarn'd againft his foe,
  And weak through feeble age ;
All hopelefs with the rav'nous wolf
  Could *Galvan* battle wage ?

Young *Edwy*, ſtartled at the din,
   Th' unequal conteſt view'd ;
Not long his gen'rous gallant ſoul
   Deliberating ſtood.

Beardleſs, defenceleſs as he was,
   Unknown to deeds of war ;
He quickly ſhew'd what native worth
   And bravery could dare.

From ſtruggling *Galvan*'s panting breaſt,
   Beſmear'd with foam and gore,
The beaſt he forc'd ; and with a craſh
   His jaws aſunder tore.

Beneath th' aſtoniſh'd hero's feet
   The wolf expiring lay,
Which threaten'd, but a moment paſt,
   To rend his life away.

Before his eyes, with graceful air,
   The blooming *Edwy* ſtood ;
Who kindly cheer'd his haraſs'd ſoul,
   And kindly ſtaunch'd his blood.

Yet, little ween'd he for whoſe ſake
   Such danger he had brav'd ;
But little ween'd how great a life
   His daring hand had ſav'd.

For though the ancient Noble's fame
   Had often reach'd his ear ;
Yet too obſcure his ſtation was,
   Before him to appear :

For *Edwy's* gentle muſing mind
   Retirement lov'd full well ;
And rarely with his compeers round
   His ſteps were ſeen to dwell :

Nor if perchance the Noble's horns
   Awak'd the neighb'ring wood,
Would he, to view the ſplendid train,
   With them his ſteps obtrude.

Yet not from ſullenneſs, or pride,
   Sprung his ſequeſter'd life ;
And leſs his temper ſweet would find
   Occaſion bad for ſtrife.

But form'd in melancholy's mould,
   Beneath the green-wood ſhade,
Unheard, unſeen, he joy'd to be
   In meditation laid :

Yet counſel kind, and ready help,
   To ev'ry neighbour ſwain,
Who ſtill ſo ready was as he,
   To lend, upon the plain ?

And much his lore they all admir'd,
   And much his goodneſs lov'd ;
And knew and priz'd that courage which
   For *Galvan* he had prov'd.

Him to his humble dwelling oft
   He kindly preſs'd to wend ;
And offer'd his ſupporting arm,
   His footſteps to attend.

D

And oft he fear'd the rav'ning wolf
  Had made a deadly wound;
And oft his linen he would rend,
  And wrap his throat around.

" Who, and what art thou ?" *Galvan* cried;
  " Relate thy birth and name,
" Whose valour foremoft ought to ftand
  " Upon the lift of fame.

" Whoever, and whate'er, thou art,
  " An heart thou haft full brave;
" And a ftout arm, which thou haft ftretch'd
  " Right well, my life to fave.

" Nor think a life of little worth
  " Hath been preferv'd by thee :
" Nor think that *Galvan* for the boon
  " Ungrateful e'er will be."

At *Galvan's* name a rofy blufh
  Suffus'd young *Edwy's* cheek ;
And downcaft eyes, and lifted hands,
  Surprife and rev'rence fpeak.

With modeft air he anfwers mild :
  " Old *Hilda's* fon I am,
" Thy vaffal, virtuous, though poor,
  " And *Edwy* is my name."

" That thou art virtuous, gen'rous, brave,"
  The Noble quick reply'd,
" Hath in thy conduct, gallant youth,
  " This day been amply try'd.

" Nor vaſſal thou, nor ſhepherd ſwain,
　" A future hour ſhall ſee;
" My lov'd companion, and my friend,
　" Henceforward ever be:

" And ſure a firmer, worthier friend,
　" No man can ever have;
" Since all unarm'd, thy life was riſk'd,
　" A ſtranger's life to ſave."

" Deteſted were the abjeƈt hand !"
　(The ſhepherd warmly cry'd,)
" That to relieve ſuch deep diſtreſs
　" Its proweſs had not try'd;

" And ever bleſſed be the day,
　" When in ſuch lucky ſtrife,
" This weak, and far unworthy arm,
　" Sav'd noble *Galvan*'s life !"

But now the ancient warrior's train
　Appearing, gather'd round,
With great amazement at the plight
　In which their lord was found.

And much their eyes young *Edwy* ſcann'd,
　And much they gaz'd to ſee
Galvan to ſuch a lowly ſwain
　Bewray ſuch courteſy:

For good as noble *Galvan* was,
　And gen'rous as his mind;
Yet ſomething unto lofty pride
　His temper was inclin'd.

Now loud he vaunts of *Edwy*'s deeds;
  And on his grateful tongue,
Unnumber'd praifes of the youth,
  Unnumber'd bleffings hung!

And as he clos'd his copious tale,
  " Behold the man," he cry'd,
" Who ftill moft honour'd fhall appear,
  " Moft lov'd, at *Galvan*'s fide!

" And as you value *Galvan*'s love,
  " Or rev'rence *Galvan*'s power;
" As you your wifhes beft would prove,
  " To blefs his waning hour;

" Let gallant *Edwy*, like himfelf,
  " Your love, your fervice fhare;
" And for his pleafure and content,
  " Nor pains, nor duty fpare:

" Nor aged *Hilda* fhall lament
  " The abfence of her fon;
" Since many an added flock and herd
  " Her fertile fields fhall own:

" Thofe fields and flocks be *Galvan*'s gift;
  " And oft her aged breaft
" Shall joy to fee her darling child
  " By pow'r and wealth carefs'd."

Right onward now to *Galvan*'s hall
  The num'rous train did ride;
And *Edwy* honour'd moft of all,
  Rode faft by *Galvan*'s fide:

By *Galvan's* fide he gently rode;
   And as the courfer fair,
With trappings gay, and carriage proud,
   Seem'd as he trod the air;

The blooming youth, though all amaz'd
   At fuch unwonted ftate,
And though in homely garb attir'd,
   Yet firm and graceful fat:

And fuch his fair demeanour was,
   And fuch his comely mien,
That all efteem'd his garb alone
   Unworthy fuch a fcene.

At *Galvan's* palace ftraight arriv'd,
   Full many a knight and peer,
Expectant of the lord's return,
   They found affembled there.

To each in turn the Baron now
   Prefents the ftranger fwain;
And while his merits rare he told,
   Applaufe burft forth amain:

Applaufe burft forth, and echo'd round
   The high and fpacious hall;
While (or to pleafe their noble hoft,
   Or warm'd at honour's call)

The courteous nobles gather'd round,
   And ardent to their breaft,
With femblance fair of truth and love,
   The blufhing *Edwy* prefs'd.

E

And much they prais'd his gallant heart,
  And much his eafy air;
And wonder'd how a ftock fo bafe
  Produc'd a fruit fo fair!

Not weeting that a garment coarfe,
  A noble mind may hide;
Nor in the cot, that virtue oft
  Delighteth to abide!

Though rough as from its native bed,
  The precious diamond's blaze,
'Midft high-wrought rubies' glowing fires,
  Yet darts fuperior rays:

So Edwy 'midft the courtly fons
  Of wealth and lofty birth
Appears; and fo eclipfes all,
  By native charms and worth:

Eclipfes all that round him ftand,
  When, lo! a brighter ftar,
Outfhining every objcct elfe,
  Doth fuddenly appear:

For who that view'd the countlefs charms
  In fweet *Edilda's* face,
Or who that view'd her lovely form,
  Adorn'd with namelefs grace,

But to that form and to that face,
  Immediate homage paid;
And found attention wholly bent
  Upon the peerlefs maid?

A flowing robe of azure dye,
　　With filver fringes grac'd,
A ruby girdle faften'd round
　　Her finely-taper'd waift;

Thence floating largely on the ground
　　In many a graceful wave,
Unto her port, if fo could be,
　　More majefty it gave:

From one bar'd fhoulder, falling loofe,
　　Of alabafter hue,
A portion of her lovely neck
　　It offer'd to the view:

And yet, as envious of the boon,
　　The filver fringe arofe,
Concealing half the kinder robe
　　Had promis'd to difclofe.

O'er her foft hands meand'ring veins
　　Of brighteft azure ftray'd;
And with the pure furrounding white,
　　A pleafing contraft made:

And where her gently-fwelling arm,
　　So polifh'd, firm, and fair,
Into the elbow moulded was
　　With fymmetry moft rare,

A ruby button, carelefs fix'd
　　Within a filver loop,
The fky-blue robe, in foldings fair,
　　Moft feemly gather'd up.

Beneath the upper loofer robe,
   A fnowy veft was feen;
Yet whiter, fofter, purer far,
   The form it hid, I ween.

An azure bufkin filver lac'd,
   Her flender ankle clad;
In fandals like her dainty feet
   Did delicately tread.

Her auburn treffes deftly hung,
   Part on her ivory neck,
And part in full waves flowing down
   Her azure garment deck:

In gather'd knots a part appear'd,
   By ftrings of pearl confin'd,
And many a foft and fhining lock
   Fair wreaths of lilies bind.

Her lips like opening rofe-buds glow'd,
   And in her fpeaking eye
A piercing brightnefs mix'd its rays
   With fenfibility.

Upon her brow high dignity,
   Enthron'd with meeknefs fair,
Moft graceful fat; and truth and fenfe
   Were fweetly blended there.

Yet fomething on her forehead fair,
   Of dread, one might efpy;
And glift'ning tears did trembling ftand,
   In either anxious eye.

So do the fhadows lovely hang
  On fome fair mountain's brow :
So do the fapphire's foften'd rays
  Through clearest cryftal fhow.

At her approach in every eye
  Pleas'd admiration hung ;
And murmurs foft of joy and love
  Flow'd copious from each tongue.

Through the divided ranks the while,
  The fweet *Edilda* went
With trembling hafte, and to her Sire
  The duteous knee fhe bent.

And while the duteous knee fhe bent,
  His hand fhe fondly prefs'd,
And with a thoufand kifles fweet
  His aged lips carefs'd.

So round fome ancient cedar doth
  The fragrant jafmine twine ;
So clafps and decks fome time-worn oak,
  The perfum'd eglantine.

A fomething of that morning's chance
  In rumours fhe had heard,
And therefore with diforder'd mien,
  To learn the truth, appear'd.

But when upon her father's breaft
  The bloody marks fhe fpy'd,
Her pulfe decay'd, and on her cheek
  Her wonted rofes dy'd.

F

But foon to eafe her lab'ring heart,
  The pearly forrows flow;
And foon her tongue its fpeech regains,
  To mitigate her woe:

" Oh! by what cruel chance," fhe cry'd,
  " Do thefe fad marks appear;
" What deadly villany hath left
  " Thefe bloody traces here?

" Quick to your dear *Edilda*'s pray'r,
  " The dreaded truth reveal:
" Nor hope, that from a love like her's
  " The worft you can conceal."

Charm'd with her tender plaints and tears,
  The Hero to his breaft,
With added love, and added joy,
  His beauteous Daughter prefs'd.

And much her troubled heart he fooths,
  And much her forrow cheers;
And often from her melting eye
  He kifs'd the falling tears.

" O! let my fweet *Edilda*'s foul
  " Be comforted," he cry'd,
" And let thofe dear, thofe lovely eyes,
  " My darling child, be dry'd!

" Nor dread thefe marks of brutal rage
  " That on my breaft I bear!
" Than all my numerous fcars in war,
  " More lov'd, more honour'd far!

" Since thefe alone to *Galvan*'s foul
  " Made known the genuine birth
" Of every generous fentiment
  " That e'er adorn'd the earth :

" Made courage, known in tender youth,
  " Beyond what veterans dare ;
" And with that courage, virtue, fenfe,
  " And modefty, moft rare !

" Thefe high endowments turn and view
  " In lowly *Edwy*'s face ;
" And let *Edilda* judge if now
  " Her Father flatter'd has :

" Ev'n let my fweet *Edilda* judge ;
  " The while from me affur'd,
" That *Edwy*'s graceful form is by
  " His merits rare obfcur'd !

" But for thofe virtues which thefe lips
  " So warmly, juftly, praife,
" Thy Father ere this hour had touch'd
  " The limit of his days."

Scarce had the words efcap'd his lips,
  Or ever fhe did fee
The blooming fhepherd at her feet
  Upon his bended knee.

His light-brown locks, in numerous curls,
  Upon his fhoulders hung ;
And round his neck his wonted fcrip
  And pipe were lightly flung.

A deepen'd colour warm'd his cheek,
  And made his forehead fair,
And brilliant eyes, with brighter beams
  And finer hue, appear.

Expreffion fweet, with fpirit high,
  Were temper'd in his face;
And through that glafs the generous foul
  Moft clearly one might trace.

His form alike with elegance
  And manly firmnefs blefs'd,
Array'd in youth's feducing bloom,
  A thoufand charms exprefs'd.

Nor could the homely ruffet coat
  Conceal his noble air;
Which rather, from the contraft wide,
  More ftriking did appear.

A moment's paufe *Edilda* made,
  The while her lovely eyes
Dwelt on the kneeling Shepherd's form,
  With pleafure and furprife.

Upon the Shepherd's form fhe gaz'd,
  Till o'er her blooming cheek
A fweet confufion made the blood
  In ftronger currents break;

There fpreading from her fpotlefs breaft
  Where rifing blufhes glow,
As when the rofy morning breaks
  Upon a hill of fnow.

Her lily hand moſt gracciouſly
   She proffers for a kiſs;
Which *Edwy* gently, trembling, touch'd,
   As worthleſs of the bliſs.

And while that ſoft and lovely hand
   His red lip preſſes ſweet,
He weens, tranſported, that the world
   Is worthleſs ſuch a treat!

" Believe, thou gallant Youth," ſhe cry'd,
   " That while *Edilda* lives,
" She muſt remember by whoſe hand
   " Her noble Sire ſurvives;

" And while remembrance of a boon,
   " So precious, I poſſeſs,
" Believe, brave Youth, my grateful heart
   " Shall thee unceaſing bleſs."

" O lady! gracious, good, and fair,"
   Th' enraptur'd Shepherd cry'd,
" To win a bleſſing from thy lips,
   " *Edwy* had willing dy'd;

" Too happy! that his feeble arm
   " Could noble *Galvan* ſave;
" And happier ſtill, of him and thee,
   " To live and die the ſlave!"

And from that day the gallant Youth
   In *Galvan*'s grateful breaſt,
Above each valued friend around,
   The deareſt place poſſeſs'd.

     G

To higheſt truſt, to faireſt ſtate,
  Was *Edwy* now preferr'd;
And quickly in the Noble's court,
  With vantage great appear'd:

For quickly to his docile mind
  Each liberal art was known,
And poliſh'd manners quickly were
  Peculiarly his own.

Yet could not favour in his breaſt
  Beget o'erweening pride;
Still humble, modeſt, gentle, good,
  'Midſt Fortune's higheſt tide.

END OF THE FIRST PART.

EDWY AND EDILDA.

PART II.

By all efteem'd, by all admir'd,
    And much by all carefs'd;
What anxious thought could now difturb
    The heav'n in *Edwy*'s breaft?

Was halcyon peace fair virtue's dow'r,
    He fure had happy been;
But good and evil in this life
    Still make a motley fcene.

Thus *Edwy*, favour'd paft his thought,
    'Midft all his bleffings found
A fecret arrow in his heart
    Inflict a deadly wound.

And who can doubt, that reads this tale,
    The fource of *Edwy*'s woe?
Who but will guefs *Edilda*'s charms,
    The fource from whence they flow?

Thofe dazzling charms with virtue join'd,
    Which Heav'n itfelf approv'd;
What marvel if the Shepherd faw,
    Admir'd, efteem'd, and lov'd?

What marvel! when his own pure heart
    The tablet was moſt fair,
Where every good and noble thought
    At large inſcribed were.

Alas! their magic pow'r he felt
    Within his artleſs breaſt,
Long ere the flame that bicker'd there,
    Was to himſelf confeſs'd.

He fondly deem'd that rev'rence high,
    Eſteem, and duty fair,
With admiration, as of Heav'n,
    Alone were center'd there.

And though with high and rare delight,
    His eyes, he knew full well,
On ſweet *Edilda*'s peerleſs face
    Unceaſing lov'd to dwell:

Although he knew his panting heart
    Upon her accents hung;
And that his melting ſoul was loſt
    In raptures, when ſhe ſung:

Yet ſtill the unexperienc'd youth
    Theſe daily tranſports prov'd;
Nor once divin'd, thoſe tranſports ſweet
    Were ſymptoms that he lov'd.

Day after day, with ſilent courſe,
    Thus fleeted faſt away;
But nothing yet to *Edwy*'s ſelf
    Did *Edwy*'s heart betray:

Mean-time, of fweet *Edilda*'s charms,
  Did all-reporting Fame
Through every province, far and near,
  The wondrous pow'r proclaim.

Hence many a Warrior of renown,
  And many a Noble great,
To *Galvan*'s palace hy'd away,
  In all the pride of ftate :

To *Galvan*'s palace quickly hy'd,
  And when admitted there,
Each one *Edilda* foon confefs'd
  The faireft of the fair.

But ftill the Virgin's gentle heart
  Each fuitor woo'd in vain ;
And ftill the hymenëal bands
  She view'd with cold difdain.

Oft her indulgent Father's lips
  Had fworn a folemn vow,
That ne'er, reluctant to the yoke,
  Her bofom he would bow.

And oft the gen'rous Warrior faid,
  His vaft poffeffions all,
His noble race and honour'd name,
  Without an heir fhould fall ;

Or ever at the altar's foot
  Edilda's eyes fhou'd wear
Averted looks, or on the bands
  Of Hymen drop one tear.

And though in fecret *Galvan* wifh'd
 His lovely Daughter's heart
Might to fome meet Adorer's fuit
 Its tendernefs impart;

Yet ftill as each his vows preferr'd,
 And quick difmiffion met,
The gen'rous Noble veil'd the cares
 Her coldnefs did beget.

The cuftom was in *Galvan's* hall,
 When each returning day,
In various kinds of manly fports,
 Was cheerful worn away;

To greet with many a dulcet ftrain
 The evening's dufky hour;
And charm the ftillnefs of the night
 With mufic's potent pow'r.

Hence every gueft whofe happy frame
 Kind Heav'n the temper fine
To feel th' expreffive founds had giv'n
 Of harmony divine,

Made, either with his vocal notes,
 The vaulted ceiling ring,
Or fwept, with many a concord fweet,
 The lyre's enchanting ftring.

As warbling wood-larks anfwer fweet,
 The tufted groves among,
While *Philomela* to the moon
 Chants her pathetic fong:

So fair *Edilda*'s plaintive notes
    Are heard tranfcending all;
And fo do *Edwy*'s mellow tones
    Swell fweetly through the hall.

But when to her melodious voice
    His pipe accords its note,
And anfwers fweet, with melting ftrains,
    The mufic of her throat;

Then harmony with rapture meets
    Each fafcinated ear,
And Silence, from the curtain'd night,
    Enchanted! ftoops to hear.

And fuch their forms, and fuch their grace,
    And fuch their fkill, that he
Apollo fitly had been deem'd,
    And fhe *Calliope*.

In England's court a Lord there was
    Of great eftate and fame;
Who high in *Egbert*'s favour dwelt,
    And *Edbald* was his name.

His age, the time when manhood firm
    Has pafs'd of youth the bloom,
Yet ftill doth promife many years
    Of luftihood to come:

His perfon portly, ftrong, and tall;
    His face was fiercely fair,
His graceful manners pleas'd, yet aw'd,
    And haughty was his air:

His nat'ral genius, quick and ſtrong,
   By ſkilful maſters taught,
With knowledge far above his peers,
   And wit, was amply fraught.

But what are all the gifts of Heav'n,
   Improv'd with earthly art,
If reaſon and bright virtue bend,
   And paſſion guides the heart?

Thus *Edbald*, though ſupremely bleſt,
   Diſdaining reaſon's ſway,
Obſcur'd the faireſt gifts of Heav'n,
   And tarniſh'd virtue's ray.

His heart impetuous, ſcornful, vain,
   Could no controlment brook ;
And deadly fury oft his ſoul,
   As with a whirlwind, ſhook.

Alas ! that overweening pride
   Should ſpoil a fruit ſo fair !
That ever paſſion ſhould deface
   A gem, ſo rich and rare !

Such *Edbald* was, by all admir'd ;
   Careſs'd, though fear'd by all ;
For ſtill to favour, pow'r, and wealth,
   Will ſervile flatt'ry fall.

But few I ween to *Edbald*'s ſelf
   Offer'd the tribute fair
Of friendſhip, free from falſehood's ſtain,
   Of faith and love ſincere.

A fpacious manor, feated near
 To Severn's winding tide,
The haughty *Edbald* had obtain'd
 When noble *Erpwald* dy'd:

For *Erpwald*, who his uncle was,
 To all his fortunes fair,
Childlefs himfelf, had left of late
 Edbald the only heir.

Attended with a fplendid train,
 He quits the court awhile;
And, to poffefs the wealth bequeath'd,
 Rides many a tedious mile:

By Severn's fide his journey wends,
 And paffing on his road,
He fudden came where *Galvan*'s tow'rs
 With ample honours ftood.

The hour ferene of evening mild,
 The dazzling glare of day,
In foft and flow-advancing fhades,
 Now filent ftole away.

The Noble paus'd, and to his fquire
 A quick commandment gives,
To afk what lord within thofe tow'rs
 So fair and ftately lives?

He hies him inftant to the gate,
 And as the horn did found,
Lord *Galvan*'s porters us'd their fpeed,
 And quickly gather'd round,

I

Soon to the courteous queſtion they
   An anſwer courteous gave:
" The honour'd *Galvan* dwelleth here,
  " Rich, noble, good, and brave!"

At *Galvan*'s name the Warrior's face
   A ſmile of pleaſure wears;
For he the aged Lord had known,
   Ev'n from his earlieſt years.

And often in his father's court,
   An infant yet in war,
Galvan his eager hand had taught
   To wield the ſword and ſpear.

" Return to honour'd *Galvan*'s gate, "
   Unto his ſquires he cry'd;
" And ſay, Earl *Edbald* means this night
  " With *Galvan* to abide."

And ſcarcely had the porters ſtrong
   Set wide the lofty gate,
When *Edbald* on his courſer gay
   Pranc'd proudly in thereat.

And ſcarce the tidings of his gueſt
   Had noble *Galvan* heard,
Or ever at his portal fair
   The puiſſant gueſt appear'd.

The ancient Hero, fill'd with joy,
   The far-fam'd Warrior meets;
And with an open heart and arm
   The honour'd Noble greets.

" Welcome, thrice welcome," loud he cry'd,
　" Is *Edbald* to my hall !
" Whatever chance has led thee here,
　" May fair that chance befal !

" And if my pow'r but mates my will,
　" Thy treatment here fhall be
" Worthy thy honour'd father's fon,
　" And worthy, Lord, of thee."

Moſt gracioufly the valiant Earl
　To *Galvan* made reply ;
And much he thank'd his greetings kind,
　And much his courtefy.

Thence to the hofpitable hall
　He pafs'd with *Galvan* ſtraight,
Where many a Knight and Baron bold
　In focial converfe fat.

And there the fweet *Edilda* too,
　With other ladies fair,
As ufual, at the dufky hour
　Of eve, affembled were.

With other ladies fair fhe fat ;
　But who, when fhe was by,
On other beauties ever glanc'd
　With an approving eye ?

The filver lyre, but lately mute,
　Within her lily hand
She lightly held ; while with his pipe,
　Edwy did graceful ſtand :

And as the accents of her voice
    He modeſt ſeem'd to wait,
On his fine face delight and love
    In glowing tranſports ſat.

But ſoon as lofty *Edbald*'s ſteps
    Approach'd the circle fair,
The whole aſſembly deftly roſe
    To do him honour there.

With noble mien he courteous bows
    To each ſaluting gueſt,
And for their courteſy, content
    And mickle thanks expreſs'd.

Lo! *Galvan*, who a moment paſt
    Had quitted *Edbald*'s ſide,
His lovely Daughter leads along,
    With all a father's pride!

To *Edbald* he preſents the maid:
    And as her accents ſweet,
With many a welcome, full, and fair,
    The noble Stranger greet;

Aſtoniſhment and rapture high
    Were mingled in his look!
And while ſhe talk'd, he ſurely ween'd
    It was an angel ſpoke!

His air ſo haughty vaniſh'd quick,
    As with an alter'd eye
And ſoften'd voice, in gallant terms,
    He ſeemly made reply.

And whilft along the fpacious hall,
   'Midft parted ranks they move;
He feems the ftately God of War,
   And fhe the Queen of Love.

By fair *Edilda* feated clofe
   At *Galvan*'s plenteous board,
A rich repaft her thoufand charms
   His dazzled eyes afford:

A rich repaft her charms afford;
   The while the various feaft,
And fparkling wines, before his eyes
   Are unregarded plac'd.

But now the filver lyre he kens,
   And afks *Edilda* fweet,
If harmony's foft touches were
   For her a pleafure meet?

At her affent the filver lyre
   He takes, and o'er its ftrings
His nimble hand, with magic touch,
   A thoufand changes rings.

Loud and more loud the fwelling chords
   Now all majeftic roll;
Soft and more foft now fink away,
   And footh, and melt the foul.

Upon his fingers finely ftrung
   With harmony, the while
Edilda's eyes were firmly fix'd
   With many a raptur'd fmile!

K

Edilda fmil'd, and all approv'd
   But one, whofe love-fick heart
Seem'd from his bofom with her fmiles
   Impatient to depart.

For while the maid delighted heard
   The fkilful *Edbald* play,
The jealous *Edwy's* wretched foul
   In mis'ry funk away.

Upon his brows a cold dew hung,
   And in his heaving breaft
The lab'ring figh, and quicken'd throb,
   An anguifh deep exprefs'd.

But foon by emulation ftung,
   While *Edbald* all admir'd,
To win an equal palm of praife,
   His fpirit high afpir'd.

And to his wifh the founding lyre
   No fooner filent ftands,
Than *Edwy* tunes his mellow pipe
   At *Galvan's* kind commands.

His pipe he tunes, and while each nerve
   The jealous Shepherd ftrains ;
Unwonted tributes of applaufe
   His new-born fkill obtains.

But *Edbald* far above the reft
   His high encomiums rung,
And wonder vaft at *Edwy's* fkill
   Flow'd copious from his tongue.

And when he learnt who *Edwy* was,
   Much marvell'd that his birth
Should fo, beyond compare, be found
   Excell'd, by wit and worth.

And much his perfon he extoll'd,
   And fwore his virtues rare,
And courtly manners, worthy well
   The higheft honours were.

But what avail thefe praifes now
   To *Edwy*'s aching heart,
Where fatal jealoufy had fix'd,
   Unfpy'd, her poifon'd dart!

When filent fleep had every gueft
   In filken flumbers laid,
In vain his poppies he would ftrew
   On *Edwy*'s haplefs head.

The conflict dire of paffions ftrong
   That ftruggled in his breaft,
His tortur'd foul and watchful eye
   Depriv'd of balmy reft.

Awhile with inward groans he tofs'd,
   In deep and fpeechlefs woe;
Nor dar'd to probe the rankling wound,
   From whence fuch evils flow.

At laft, unable to contain
   The guft of grief, he cry'd,
" Ah! would to God that *Edwy* ere
   " This fatal night had dy'd!

" Accurfed be my feeble pipe,
    " That could not once infpire
" The fweet regards, that waited ftill
    " On *Edbald*'s tuneful lyre.

" Ah! what avails his hated praife,
    " When fair *Edilda*'s fmile,
" That wonted tribute to my lays,
    " Which did my heart beguile,

" Unto his better, happier hand
    " A higher tribute paid;
" And round her lips, at *Edbald*'s lays,
    " So long, fo fweetly play'd?

" But, wretched fhepherd, why fhould'ft thou
    " Lament his fweeter ftrain?
" And why, of bright *Edilda*'s fmiles
    " Should one like thee complain?

" What mad prefumption thus thy heart
    " With impulfe ftrange can move?
" Ah! can it be! almighty powers!
    " It *is*, it *muft* be love!"

This fatal truth, fo long conceal'd
    In *Edwy*'s fecret breaft,
Too late difclos'd! with tenfold woe
    The wretched youth oppreft.

Impatient longings, fierce defires,
    The throws of wild defpair,
With jealoufy's tormenting pangs,
    Made dreadful havock there.

The alter'd *Edwy*, late the pride
    Of *Galvan's* crowded hall,
No longer anfwer'd jocund now
    At mirth's convivial call:

The unfrequented path he fought,
    And there he lov'd alone
To pour his forrows on the earth,
    And heave the bitter groan.

While others ftill in various fports
    Confum'd the cheerful day,
To folitude and racking woe
    He gave himfelf away.

But when the hour of ev'ning came,
    Then what was *Edwy's* care?
How was his haplefs bofom torn
    By love, and by defpair!

'Gainft nature ftill in hateful mirth
    Conftrain'd to bear a part;
Yet hear that tongue, and meet thofe eyes,
    That pierc'd him to the heart.

But when at fweet *Edilda's* word
    The tuneful pipe he takes,
And with the mufic of her voice,
    Soft melody awakes;

O then his gentle amorous heart
    Feels moft love's fubtle fire;
And while he plays, his very foul
    Seems melting with defire.

A change fo great in one fo lov'd,
  Not long could be conceal'd,
While pallid looks and fpirits broke
  The private pangs reveal'd.

Soon *Galvan*, with a friendly care,
  Intreats the drooping Swain
To fay, what fecret difcontent
  Or ficknefs caus'd his pain.

What difcontent in *Galvan*'s court,
  So bleft with *Galvan*'s love ?
He anfwers mild, " Can *Edwy*'s heart
  " With bafeft influence move ?

" With lurking malady alone
  " His grateful heart's oppreft ;
" And cafe and cheerfulnefs are driven,
  " With health, from *Edwy*'s breaft."

The fkilful leeches fummon'd now,
  Their utmoft aid impart ;
But all in vain ! the evil lay
  Beyond the reach of art.

Meantime the fweet *Edilda*'s eyes
  In *Edwy*'s alter'd face,
And languid fpirits, quickly faw
  The fatal change there was.

She faw, and mourn'd ; for paffing well
  She priz'd the gentle youth,
For pleafing converfe, talents rare,
  For modefty and truth :

And of his welfare fhe inquir'd
    Full oft, with tender care;
And watch'd his cheek, and griev'd to fee
    The rofes dying there.

No more fhe joy'd to hear the lyre
    By *Edbald* nimbly fwept:
And when he urg'd his tender fuit,
    She only figh'd and wept.

She figh'd and wept; for well fhe knew
    Her honour'd Father's heart,
In *Edbald*'s vows, and *Edbald*'s pains,
    Still bore an anxious part.

By love arrefted, *Edbald*'s fteps
    In *Galvan*'s court had ftay'd;
And all his thoughts had center'd long
    In the enchanting maid.

But fore the haughty Lord was touch'd,
    To find his proffer'd love
In fair *Edilda*'s adverfe breaft
    No foft return could move.

And oft indignant he had vow'd
    To pay her fcorn with fcorn:
But ftill the pow'r of mighty love
    Such vows had overborn.

Convinc'd at laft that all his pride
    To combat love was vain,
He hopes, from time and tender care,
    His wifhes to obtain.

The generous *Galvan* too, her heart
   By foothing foft would move,
And mild perfuafion's pow'rful voice,
   To fmile on *Edbald*'s love.

Yet ftill the coy determin'd maid
   Rejected all his pray'rs;
And clofely prefs'd, would urge his vow,
   And bind it with her tears.

With inward grief fhe mark'd the while
   Poor *Edwy*'s faft decay;
And figh'd to fee fo fair a flow'r
   So early fade away.

One evening as he trembling ftood,
   And with his pipe fo clear,
Accompanied her melting notes,
   That all were charm'd to hear;

The tears, unheeded, from his cheek
   Dropt frequent on the book
Where fweet *Edilda*'s lovely eyes
   Attentively did look.

She heard them fall, fhe faw them moift,
   Upon the notes fhe fung;
While pity throb'd within her breaft,
   And trembled on her tongue:

But ending now, fhe fudden turn'd
   With fweet and tender air,
And pray'd, in whifpers foft, to know
   The caufe of *Edwy*'s care.

" Afk not," he cry'd, " the fatal caufe
" From whence my forrows flow.
" O! afk not what I ne'er muft fpeak,
" Nor you fhould ever know."

He added not, and from her turn'd,
　Diftrefs'd, his glowing cheek,
While foft involuntary fighs
　Her fecret anguifh fpeak.

Yet ftill th' emotion foft to hide,
　She us'd her utmoft care:
Nor dar'd once queftion her fond heart,
　What paffions wreftled there.

A cuftom was in *Egbert*'s court,
　When bloody wars did ceafe,
And doughty warriors arms were laid
　Upon the lap of peace;

Left warlike arms and pow'rs fhould ruft,
　To mark the lifted field,
Where Heroes, fam'd for val'rous deeds,
　The glittering lance might wield.

Nor fame alone, nor love of arms,
　Their beating bofoms fir'd,
A fofter paffion oft their hearts
　More ardently infpir'd.

Hence many a Knight and Baron bold
　Had borne the envied prize,
Encourag'd by th' approving glance
　Of fome kind beauty's eyes.

M

But ftill within the lifted field,
  For prowefs, none could dare
With noble *Edbald*'s matchlefs might
  Prefumptuous! to compare.

Lo! at his wifh his noble hoft
  Invites, both far and nigh,
Each valiant Knight and Baron bold
  To deeds of Chivalry.

For *Edbald* held a fecret hope,
  That, with high deeds of fame,
His arm in fweet *Edilda*'s breaft
  Might roufe the fleeping flame.

The Heralds foon to all around,
  The tidings loud declare;
And fay, " the Victors choice rewards
  " With honour great fhall wear.

" The firft in might *Edilda*'s hand
  " A coftly fword fhall give,
" With golden hilt of curious work.
  " The fecond fhall receive

" A brightly-polifh'd ebon bow,
  " With filver ringlets grac'd;
" And in the bow a taper fhaft
  " Of filver, featly plac'd."

Quickly doth many a Warrior brave
  His goodly arms prepare;
And weens with glory in the lifts
  To poife the pond'rous fpear.

But *Edbald*, far beyond them all,
  His anxious cares addreſt ;
For valour, glory, pride, and love,
  All burnt within his breaſt.

The roſy morn now bluſhes bright,
  When many a deed of fame,
Emblazon'd fair in honour's field,
  Shall grace the Hero's name.

The ſpace is mark'd, the feats are fix'd ;
  And ſoon the ladies fair,
A goodly train ! in bright array,
  Aſſembling, reſted there.

With *Galvan* ſat the Lords and Knights,
  Whoſe valour feeble age
Forbad the glorious tournament
  With vigorous youth to wage.

High in the centre, underneath
  A gorgeous canopy,
The fair *Edilda* charm'd each heart,
  And dazzled every eye.

Sweet wreaths of roſes bind her hair
  With many a fragrant twine,
And purple robes, and jewels bright,
  To deck her charms combine.

Than purple robes, or jewels bright,
  Her charms more ſhining far ;
Nor could the roſes with her cheeks,
  Nor with her breath compare !

Upon her knees the bow was laid,
  One Victor's fair reward;
And in her hand fhe graceful held
  The coftly glittering fword.

Yet penfive languors fomewhat dull'd
  The brightnefs of her eye;
And oft her fnowy breaft appear'd
  To heave a gentle figh.

For wretched *Edwy*'s mournful words,
  Still founded in her ear;
And much fhe mourn'd, where glory call'd,
  That *Edwy* was not there:

His abfence mourn'd from honour's field;
  But more the cankering tooth
Of forrow, that withheld him thence,
  And blighted fore his youth.

The trumpets found, the barriers ope;
  And in the lifts appear
Full many a Champion, mounted bold
  Upon his courfer fair.

Their armour fhines, they point the lance,
  Their nimble courfers bound;
And with a firm and warlike air
  They prance the lifts around.

Forthwith a Pageantry moft rare
  Engages every eye,
Where Arms, and Steeds, and Warriors fhew
  With mickle bravery.

A gallant Champion heads the train,
　Upon a milk-white fteed,
Whofe gilded trappings glitter bright
　About his tofling head.

And now his arched neck he bows
　On his broad bofom fair,
Now proudly fnorting champs his bit,
　And fnuffs the ambient air.

His eager eye-balls glow with fire,
　And while he thunders round,
His golden fhoes, with paces high,
　Spurn as they touch the ground.

The puiffant Warrior on his back
　All fiercely graceful rode;
And fhook his lance, till chilling fear
　Ran fhiv'ring through their blood.

His armour fplendid was to view,
　Of polifh'd fteel and gold;
And with a mighty hand he ftill
　His fiery fteed control'd.

Upon his polifh'd helmet high
　The fpangled plumage fhone;
And flowing half-way down his back,
　Wav'd fparkling to the fun.

Upon his fhield, in rare device!
　Was feen a Painting brave,
Where Love, the Palm of Valour to
　A kneeling Warrior gave.

N

Above in golden letters bright,
  Thefe words were feen the while ;
" Love, thou art juft !" and thefe beneath,
  " I conquer by thy fmile."

A numerous train his fteps attend,
  And round the lifted field,
In fhining pairs behind him rank'd,
  A goodly profpect yield.

But as the Warrior paft the place
  Where fweet *Edilda* fhone,
With couched lance, in fair falute,
  He graceful bow'd him down :

And as the beaver he did lift,
  His face was well defcry'd ;
And *Edbald's* high renowned name
  Was heard on every fide.

The trumpets found a fprightly charge,
  The tilters take their ftand,
And wait with ardent throbbing breafts,
  The clarion's laft command.

It fhrilly founds ; and now amain,
  Along the quaking ground,
The champions rufh ; they furious clafh ;—
  And clanging arms refound.

Full many a Warrior of renown
  On that redoubted day,
With batter'd mail, and bruifed limbs,
  In duft low grov'ling lay.

But ſtill above each tilter brave,
  Earl *Edbald* glorious ſhone;
And each encounter more declar'd
  The envied prize his own.

At length as round he proudly wheel'd
  With fierce and ſcornful air,
He ween'd that no advent'rous Knight
  Would further conteſt dare.

But vainly ween'd! for once again
  The martial trumpets found;
And once again a rival Knight
  Appear'd within the bound.

And much his form, and motions much,
  Attracted every eye;
And in his mien a ſpirit rare,   .
  And grace, one might eſpy.

Upon a coal-black ſteed he rode,
  That like the ebon ſhone;
And all his armour wore the face
  Of one quite woe-begone.

For all of black his armour was,
  But where upon his breaſt,
A bleeding heart quite pierced through,
  His malady expreſt.

And round the heart, in curious guiſe,
  This motto did appear,
In flaming letters portray'd bright;
  " I love, and I deſpair !"

The clarions found,—like rufhing winds
   The courfers wing their way;
And at their mighty fhock each breaft
   Is fill'd with ftrange difmay;

At the fierce ftroke of *Edbald*'s fpear,
   The fable Warrior reel'd,
But with his blow the puiffant Earl
   Lay ftretch'd upon the field.

Each bofom at the Hero's might
   Is fill'd with vaft furprife,
And long applaufes echo round,
   And rend the vaulted fkies.

Another, and another yet,
   Within the lifted field,
The fable Warrior's thund'ring arm
   Reluctant forc'd to yield.

At length, to hail the trumpet's voice,
   Thrice founding far and near,
No Champion to conteft the prize
   Of valour, durft appear.

To fweet *Edilda*'s judgment-feat,
   The victor now they lead,
Where of his prowefs from her hand,
   He, kneeling, takes the meed.

And while the coftly glittering fword
   She gracioufly beftows;
" May this," fhe cried, " defend thee ftill,
   " And ftill offend thy foes!"

The Warrior bow'd with mickle grace;
   And as he touch'd her hand,
No longer could his lab'ring breaſt
   Its fervours ſtrong command.

" All-honour'd maid!'' (in tranſports loſt)
   " By thy dear hand," he cry'd,
" While life remains, this envied ſword
   " Shall honour *Edwy's* ſide."

The words were paſt without recall;
   Deep bluſhes warm her cheek,
While from her faint and fault'ring tongue
   Theſe trembling accents break:

" Why, *Edwy,* why doſt thou perſiſt
   " To wound my tender heart?—
" But time is ſhort; hence, quickly hence;
   " Unſeen, unheard, depart.

" *Edilda* would not for the world
   " It ever ſhould appear,
" That noble *Edbald* was o'erthrown
   ", By lowly *Edwy's* ſpear."

" Fear not," in whiſpers ſoft, he cry'd,
   " That *Edwy* ſhall be known
" To any eye that views him here
   " But thine, ſweet maid, alone."

" Nor had *Edilda Edwy* found,
   " Had not his treach'rous tongue,
" And treach'rous heart, the purpos'd cloud
   " Diſpell'd, that round him hung."

o

With low obeifance, fighing, now
   He quits *Edilda*'s feet,
And, like a fhadow, from the lifts,
   Unknown, doth fwiftly fleet.

Edbald the while, whofe haughty foul
   Was fill'd with rage and fhame,
Curfes the arm whofe deadly force
   Had fullied his bright fame.

Behold, with fierce indignant mien,
   Sunk eye, and low'ring brows,
To meet the fecond prize decreed,
   Before the maid he bows.

The ebon bow fhe graceful gives,
   And arrow ftraight and fair;
And foothing tells how much the prize
   Beneath his merits are.

" The prize by thy beloved hand
   " Is precious made," he cry'd;
" But ere Earl *Edbald* faw this day,
   " 'Twere better he had dy'd;

" Since at the hour when moft he wifh'd
   " Bright Fame to bear away,
" At that accurfed hour alone,
   " His laurels knew decay.

" O! let this hand the champion meet
   " Once more, ye Powers above!
" Then mortal conflict fhall the force
   " Of *Edbald*'s vengeance prove.

" Then what it is to roufe my rage,
　" The trembling wretch fhall find;
" Then fhall his blood, to heal my fame,
　" Be fcatter'd to the wind!"

Forthwith the whole affembly rofe,
　And willing turn'd their feet
Where *Galvan's* tables (lordly fpread)
　The harafs'd fpirits greet.

And there around the fpicy bowls
　They focial chat away,
According to their feveral thoughts,
　The fortunes of the day.

But ftill the valiant Stranger's name
　All curious are to know ;
And ftill from each impartial tongue
　His well-earn'd praifes flow.

END OF THE SECOND PART.

EDWY AND EDILDA.

PART III.

EDWY, the while, apart retir'd,
  His lonely pillow preſt,
A thouſand cares diſtracting wide
  The empire of his breaſt.

A ſecret pleaſure each kind look,
  And every gracious word
Of ſweet *Edilda*, in the liſts,
  His muſing mind afford.

Her ſoft confuſion, tender fears,
  In dear remembrance riſe;
And Hope begins to warm his check,
  And ſparkle in his eyes.

But ſcarce ſhe flaſhes through the night,
  That hangs about his heart,
Ere fell deſpair the welcome gueſt
  Conſtraineth to depart.

" Preſumptuous wretch!" he ſighing cries,
  " What madneſs thus can move
" Thy ſoul to harbour but a thought
  " Of bright *Edilda*'s love!

" The generous maid's emotions soft,
    " From pity rose alone;
" Though by that pity *Edwy*'s heart
    " Is but the more undone.

" Or *should* a phrenfy, like thy own,
    " Her tender breaft beguile,
" Upon thy ill-condition'd love
    " To caft a fav'ring fmile;

" Could'ft thou, ungenerous! from the height
    " Where brightly fhe doth fhine,
" *Could'ft* thou debafe the noble maid
    " To fuch a ftate as thine?

" Could'ft thou, ungenerous youth! confent
    " From honour to depart,
" In *Galvan*'s breaft a viper prove,
    " And fting him to the heart?

" Let gratitude the monftrous thought
    " Within thy breaft control;
" And every noble impulfe drive
    " Such bafenefs from thy foul!

" No! tortur'd as this bofom is,
    " Yet *Edwy* ftill fhall be
" Virtuous, amidft the worft extremes
    " Of all his mifery!"

The generous purpofe feems awhile
    His anguifh to appeafe;
And fcatters through his bofom's gloom
    A few bright rays of peace:
                P

For lovely innocence alone
   The talent rare can know,
To lighten, with a radiant ſmile,
.   The dark abyſs of woe.

But quick the momentary gleam
   From *Edwy's* boſom fleets;
And *Edbald,* like a fiend of hell,
   His wild idea meets.

Frantic, he cries, " Can *Edwy's* ſoul
   " That dreadful moment bear,
" When *Edbald's* bliſs ſhall drive it on
   " To tortures, and deſpair !

" Yet, why ſhould this ungenerous heart
   " Repine at *Edbald's* bliſs ?
" Why the poor wreck ſhould that deſtroy
   " Of *Edwy's* ſhatter'd peace ?

" His pow'r, his honours, wealth, and worth,
   " His perſon, his high name;
" All, *all,* to ſweet *Edilda's* hand
   " A title large proclaim.

" Why, why then did my jealous ſoul,
   " Vain to ſubdue his might,
" In ſecret ſeek the liſted field,
   " Beneath the maſk of night?

" Did not that veil a purpoſe dark
   " To every heart betray ?
" Elſe why diſguis'd ſhould *Edwy* ſhun
   " The tell-tale eye of day ?

" Why, proudly, did I wifh to fhine
 " In fweet *Edilda's* eyes?
" Why from her noble Suitor wifh,
 " Bafely, to win the prize?

" Why does the bold ungenerous deed
 " Not now difpleafe my heart?
" And why the Warrior's fullied fame
 " An envious joy impart?

" O let me hafte from *Galvan's* court
 " The fpoiler to remove,
" That blights the wifhes of his heart,
 " And cankers *Edbald's* love!

" Then fhall *Edilda's* kinder eye
 " Her worthier lover blefs;
" And noble *Galvan's* generous foul
 " Its whole defire poffefs.

" Yet once again, before my heart
 " In folitude forlorn,
" Th' eternal lofs of all it loves
 " Shall unremitting mourn;

" Yet once again, *Edilda's* charms
 " Shall blefs poor *Edwy's* fight,
" Before his eye-lids wifh to clofe
 " In everlafting night.

" O! may the Pow'rs above for her
 " A happier lot prepare!
" O! may fhe ne'er, like *Edwy*, know
 " To love, and to defpair!"

The haplefs Youth in ufelefs plaints,
   Thus paft the night away;
And rofe, difpirited and pale,
   At morn's returning ray.

In happier days, when halcyon peace
   The gliding moments bleft,
Nor *Edwy* kenn'd the lurking fhaft
   That rankled in his breaft:

At times, beneath a blooming bow'r,
   That hid the eye of day,
At fweet *Edilda's* bidding he
   His tuneful pipe would play.

'Midft fummer's heats *Edilda* ftill
   The paftime much approv'd;
And who can doubt that what fhe lik'd
   Th' empaffion'd *Edwy* lov'd ?

A winding row of fringed elms
   Led to the cool retreat,
Whofe rugged trunks were circled by
   The pea and woodbine fweet.

The bow'r itfelf, a little heav'n
   Of various fweets compofe,
Where jafmines and the fragrant brier
   Would emulate the rofe,

Nor eglantines were wanting there,
   Nor myrtles odorous green,
Which form'd a feemly contraft to
   The flow'rs that blufh'd between.

Sweet flowrets of a thousand dyes
    Enamell'd thick the ground,
And with the bow'r's soft perfume vy'd
    To scent the air around.

Here each plum'd warbler of the grove
    With envy stretch'd his throat,
To rival *Edwy*'s dulcet strains,
    With many a liquid note.

While the clear brook, that winding flow'd
    Beside the calm retreat,
Its lulling gurglings join'd to form
    A music strangely sweet.

Not Eden's self a fairer spot
    Could boast 'midst all her bow'rs,
What time calm innocence repos'd
    On beds of fragrant flow'rs.

The hapless *Edwy*, at the hour
    Of fresh and dewy morn,
To this sequester'd spot his steps
    Unweetingly did turn.

Unweetingly his steps he turn'd;
    For, lost in woe, his mind
Rul'd not his feet, which thitherward
    From habitude inclin'd.

Not so *Edilda*'s, who had ris'n
    At earliest dawn of day,
And to the bow'r with *purpos'd* step,
    Had softly sped away.

Q

Unto her favourite bow'r she fped;
   For there she thought alone,
Unfeen, unheard, to drop the tear,
   And heave th' unftinted groan.

A fad conftraint the evening paft,
   Her tender heart had found,
Which labour'd with a load of grief
   Amidft the mirth around.

Each ardent glance of *Edbald*'s eye
   Shot poifon in her breaft ;
And new difguft deform'd each word
   He tenderly addrefs'd.

But when the founds of *Edwy*'s praife
   Ran murmuring through the hall,
The pulfe that flutter'd in each vein,
   Confefs'd her bofom's thrall.

Too well she gather'd whence her heart
   Such jarring paffions move ;
Felt thofe were born of bitter hate,
   And thefe of gentle love.

In vain, beneath the cope of night,
   Her downy couch she prefs'd ;
Long had it loft its filken pow'r
   To feal her eyes in reft.

Yet ftill in filence she endur'd;
   Nor, though she felt the fmart,
Dar'd from her breaft attempt to tear
   The deep inflicted dart :

So fome poor wretch a barbed fhaft
  Bears from the mortal fray ;
Yet from his bofom fears to draw
  What drinks his life away.

Upon th' enamell'd turf fhe lay,
  Within the fragrant bow'r;
Of all the lovely flow'rs around,
  Herfelf the lovelieft flow'r.

Her loofen'd robes had carelefs left
  Her bofom quite reveal'd,
Had not the treffes copious flow'd,
  And half its fnow conceal'd.

Yet now and then a whifpering breeze
  O'er the light locks would blow,
Bewraying through their gloffy threads
  The paradife below.

Upon her elbow penfively
  The beauteous maiden leant;
Her lily hand upheld her head:
  The while her eyes were bent

Upon the fatal book, which ftill
  In one well-noted place,
With haplefs *Edwy's* frequent tears,
  All ftain'd and blotted was.

And as the dear yet dreaded page
  Her fad eyes ponder'd o'er,
A thoufand tears would quickly fall,
  Where one had fall'n before.

Upon the moment, *Edwy*'s feet
  Approach'd the weeping Fair;
And much his wonder was to fee
  Her beauties refting there.

A thoufand wild and clafhing thoughts
  His beating bofom move,
Divided 'twixt defire and fear,
  'Twixt reverence and love.

But what affliction rives his heart,
  When the fweet maid appears,
As nigh he fteals, with faded cheek,
  And all diffolv'd in tears !

What ftrong emotions heav'd his breaft!
  As movingly fhe cry'd,
" Ere *Edwy* came, O! would to God,
  " *Edilda,* thou hadft dy'd !"

No more his agonizing heart
  Its paffions could command,
Before her feet he caft him down;
  And while he touch'd her hand,

" O! would to God," he fobbing cry'd,
  " That *Edwy* on his bier
" Had cold been ftretch'd, or ere he coft
  " Thofe lovely eyes one tear!"

Aftonifh'd to behold the youth,
  Edilda inftant rofe ;
Blufhing, as when the dewy morn
  With humid luftre glows.

And as the pearly drops that fell
　Down her warm cheek, fhe dry'd;
With fweet, but yet majeſtic air,
　Thus gracefully reply'd:

" Rife, *Edwy!* rife, unhappy Youth!
　" And fince by chance alone,
" My tongue impell'd, hath weetlefs made
　" My guarded paſſion known;

" *Edilda* fcorns beneath deceit
　" Her fentiments to hide;
" Nor would a refuge meanly feek,
　" From bafhfulnefs, or pride.

" Yes, *Edwy*, yes, this throbbing heart
　" Feels all thy merits rare;
" Upon this bofom all thy charms
　" Too deeply graven are.

" Yet, if *Edilda* well thou know'ſt,
　" A thought will never be
" Infpir'd of this, unworthy her,
　" Nor yet unworthy thee.

" Then fearlefs tell the tender tale
　" That throbs within thy breaſt;
" So, with the temper of thy love,
　" Its worth fhall ſtand confefs'd.

" O! much *Edilda*'s thoughts have err'd,
　" If aught is there conceal'd,
" That to the world's malignant eye
　" Might dread to be reveal'd."

R

" Tranfcendant Maid!" the Youth return'd,
   " There wanted only this
" Quite to deftroy the poor remains
   " Of wretched *Edwy*'s blifs!

" Alas! had Love his deadly fhaft
   " Fix'd in this breaft alone;
" It ftill, amidft my fharpeft pangs,
   " A gleam of joy had known.

" At diftance, ftill my foul had dwelt
   " On fweet *Edilda*'s blifs;
" And from her day of joy deriv'd
   " Some glimmerings of peace.

" Yes, noble Maid, from the firft hour
   " Thefe eyes beheld thy charms,
" My beating bofom deeply felt
   " The force of love's alarms.

" Yet unexperienc'd as I was,
   " I knew not my own heart,
" Till lynx-ey'd jealoufy at length
   " Betray'd the lurking dart.

" From that fad moment was my foul
   " A prey to dire defpair,
" The while my alter'd cheek confefs'd
   " Some mifchief ftruggled there.

" Alas! 'twas this, and this alone,
   " The purpofe wild could move,
" To rend from noble *Edbald*'s hand
   " The envied prize of Love.

" But when upon my fecret bed
　" My motives lay reveal'd;
" Nor longer could my inmoft foul
　" Be from my eye conceal'd:

" Then, *then,* my jealoufy fhow'd rank
　" Beneath the confcious night;
" And all my mad prefumption ftood
　" Confefs'd before my fight.

" And whilft ingratitude and art,
　" With envy, dark and foul,
" Too plain I faw, their dwelling had
　" In my polluted foul;

" With horror ftruck, I firmly fwore
　" The fpoiler to remove,
" That blafted noble *Galvan*'s peace,
　" And canker'd *Edbald*'s love.

" Hence have my fteps bewilder'd trod,
　" At morning's dewy hour;
" And hence, unweetingly they ftray'd
　" Befide this fragrant bow'r.

" O! never more beneath its fhade
　" Shall happy *Edwy* play
" With jocund pipe, at thy beheft,
　" The noontide hour away!

" Nor ever at the clofe of eve,
　" By fair *Edilda*'s fide,
" Shall *Edwy* fwell, to mate her voice,
　" His notes, with mickle pride!

" The hours of peace for ever fled !
  " To rocks and woods alone
" His grief fhall flow ; and there, at laft,
  " In peace fhall lay him down.

" Yet 'midft the throes of fell defpair,
  " His heart a joy would prove,
" To know thy bofom felt no more
  " The pangs of hopelefs love."

His tears and fighs now choak'd his fpeech,
  The while *Edilda*'s foul
Its vaft conflicting paffions feem'd
  Unequal to control.

At length with fervour fhe reply'd,
  While down her lovely face,
The filent tears, in burfling drops,
  Each other fwiftly chafe :

" Nobly hath *Edwy* to my foul
  " His worthinefs approv'd ;
" And juftify'd *Edilda*'s heart,
  " In ftooping, where it lov'd.

" Yes, *Edwy !* *now*, with pride, my tongue
  " Its paffion fhall confefs,
" Though that ill-fated paffion fure
  " No fav'ring ftar will blefs !

" For well my noble Father's worth,
  " Yet well his pride I know ;
" Full well I ken the debt to him,
  " And to myfelf I owe.

" He never in the hour of care
  " Shall curfe *Edilda*'s name,
" For fullying, with unequal bands,
  " The luftre of his fame.

" Nor fhall his blood, fo highly priz'd,
  " I fwear by duty ! be,
" Whatever mifery is my doom,
  " Difhonour'd *firft* in me.

" Yet think not thy *Edilda*'s heart
  " Inconftant e'er will prove ;
" Think not this bofom can abjure
  " Who warm'd it firft to love.

" Never fhall haughty *Edbald*'s ear
  " This foft confeffion know ;
" Nor ever at the altar's foot,
  " To Hymen will I bow.

" Enough is given to cruel pride,
  " And duty too fevere ;
" No rival ever fhall fupplant
  " Thy lovely image here."

She ceas'd. He, fighing, thus return'd :
  " Exalted, generous Fair !
" The tribute thou would'ft pay my love,
  " Far too exalted were.

" Recall thy vow : Thy Father's years
  " Let thy fair offspring charm ;
" And may their growing virtues long
  " His aged bofom warm.

s

" O ! let not, for a wretch like me,
    " A race fo noble ceafe ;
" O ! lay thy Father's filver hairs
    " Within the grave in peace !

" I afk but this !---to kifs thy hand
    " Before I wretched go
" For ever hence !---Soft, fhe reply'd,
    " Fond lovers part not fo.

" Upon my lips thy laft adieus
    " Moft freely fhalt thou feal ;
" And on thefe faithful lips, till death,
    " Thofe dear adieus fhall dwell.

" In vain thy gentle, generous foul
    " My fix'd refolves would move :
" No other tongue fhall charm my ear,
    " Or footh my heart to love."

On her foft lips the trembling lips
    Of *Edwy* gently dwell ;
And thence with many a preffure fweet,
    Take many a fweet farewel.

" Thou darling youth," fhe weeping cry'd,
    " Why fhould we ever part ?
" But it *muft* be ; yet ftill with thee
    " Shall dwell *Edilda*'s heart."

Then mingling kiffes, tears, and fighs,
    One laft adieu they take,
And from each other's circling arms,
    In fpeechlefs forrow break.

Unto her couch, half dead with grief,
  The sweet *Edilda* stole;
And there in private utter'd all
  The anguish of her soul.

Poor *Edwy* by a different path
  Fast to his chamber hies;
And there awhile upon his bed,
  Abforb'd in forrow, lies.

At length a chofen friend he feeks,
  And to his faithful breaft,
With many a pity-moving figh,
  His wretched ftate confefs'd.

Then begs a rough difguife, ere morn,
  His friendfhip would fupply;
In which, unheeded, he might pafs
  From every prying eye.

For ere the filent fhades of night
  Were wholly paft away,
He meant from noble *Galvan's* court
  Eternally to ftray.

A letter too he prays his friend
  Would give to *Galvan's* hand,
What time he aught of *Edwy's* health
  Should on the morn demand.

For ftill the grateful Baron's heart
  Had fhown affection fair
To the fad youth, and made his health
  The fubject of his care.

The generous *Ofred* freely fwore,
  His friendfhip would fulfil,
With care exact, the utmoft fcope
  Of honour'd *Edwy*'s will.

And much his fortune he deplores,
  And much laments to fee
His fair eftate fo foon deftroy'd
  By Love's fevere decree.

For *Galvan* now the haplefs youth,
  With trembling hand, prepares
This fad epiftle, which he bath'd,
  While writing, with his tears:

" From *Galvan*'s court, by fortune hard,
  " For ever forc'd to wend;
" O! let not *Galvan*'s gen'rous foul
  " The ftrange refolve offend.

" Nor let his kindnefs ever feek
  " The caufe of *Edwy*'s woe;
" Which fits not, or his pen to write,
  " Nor *Galvan*'s heart to know.

" Yet 'midft the fhades of folitude,
  " And pangs of wild defpair,
" A grateful fenfe of *Galvan*'s love
  " Shall *Edwy*'s bofom bear.

" Nor from that love, nor thefe blefs'd feats,
  " Would *Edwy* e'er depart;
" But that he dreads to plunge a fword
  " In noble *Galvan*'s heart.

" O! may that godlike heart ne'er feel
" The pangs of deep diſtreſs;
" But from the gracious hand of Heaven
" Its whole deſire poſſeſs!"

Scarce was the cruel taſk perform'd,
　　Ere one his chamber ſought;
Who from the aged Warrior's ſelf
　　This friendly meſſage brought:

" The gallant *Edwy*, well belov'd,
" May every good befal!
" His preſence much doth *Galvan* wiſh
" To grace the mirthful hall."

" All honour to the noble Lord,"
　　The ſighing youth return'd;
And his forc'd abſence from the hall
　　By adverſe ſickneſs mourn'd.

The anſwer all unwelcome was
　　To generous *Galvan's* ear;
And much the ſickly youth he wail'd
　　To all that round him were.

From thence occaſion fair he took,
　　Upon th'enſuing morn,
To wiſh the pleaſures of the chaſe,
　　With merry hound and horn;

To wiſh the pleaſures of the chaſe,
　　Within the ſelf-fame wood,
Where firſt he in his deep diſtreſs
　　The gallant Shepherd view'd.

T

For ſtill the ſpot, with mickle pride,
 The Noble lov'd to trace;
And to his honour'd gueſt would fain
 Bewray the noted place.

The fair *Edilda*, too, he vows,
 To pleaſure *Edbald*'s heart,
Shall in the coming morning's ſports
 Bear an unwonted part.

Nor ſhe diſſents; for oft her breaſt
 A ſecret wiſh had held,
To view the ſpot where *Edwy*'s hand
 The furious wolf had quell'd.

What, though for ever from her ſight
 The Youth was forc'd to fly?
She knew the place that grac'd his name
 Muſt gratify her eye.

Meantime the truſty *Oſred*'s hand
 The ruſtic garb prepares;
Which to his friend, with falling night,
 Though loth, he ſafely bears.

Juſt as her ſable veil was ting'd
 With twilight's ſober ray,
Clad like a goatherd, with his pipe
 Poor *Edwy* ſtole away.

His favour high, and fortunes fair,
 Fair robes, and arms, forſakes;
Save that beneath his homely coat
 The valued ſword he takes.

For what was favour now to him ?
　Or what his fortunes fair ?
Edilda loft ! the world had been
　No object worth his care.

From noble *Galvan*'s lofty gate
　Reluctantly he wends ;
And to the aged *Hilda*'s farm
　His heavy travel bends.

For ftill to *Hilda*, 'midft his ftate,
　All honour he had paid ;
Nor had his heart with fortune's fmiles,
　From duty ever ftray'd.

And though he wifh'd to wander far
　From fcenes of former blifs,
He meant to paufe till filent death
　Had feal'd her eyes in peace.

Not long the Sun's refulgent beams
　Had gladden'd Nature's face,
Ere wretched *Edwy*'s weary feet
　Their native woodlands trace.

Then as the fteepy rock he view'd
　That nodded o'er the plain,
Where he was wont, in happier days,
　To pipe his carelefs ftrain ;

A thoufand fond ideas rufh
　Upon his lab'ring foul ;
And for a while, with magic power,
　His wandering fteps control.

" Ah! would to God my heart," he cry'd,
  " A joy had never known,
" Paſſing what yon ſequeſter'd ſhade
  " And ſteepy rock have ſhown!

" Ah! would to God, with calm content,
  " I thither now could ſtray;
" And, recklefs of the pangs of love,
  " Paſs with my pipe the day!

" E'en yet, forlorn as *Edwy* is,
  " His ſteps once more ſhall trace,
" And weary body reſt once more
  " Upon the well-known place."

So ſome unhappy ſpright at times
  From its dark priſon wends,
And to the ſcenes of former bliſs
  Its courſe at midnight bends.

But vainly *Edwy* ſtrives to reſt
  Beneath the once-lov'd ſhade;
The pleaſant ſpot his grief had now
  A dreary deſert made.

Ah! deadly potency of grief,
  Which every object fair,
'Gainſt Nature, its own gloomy face
  Can ſtill compel to wear!

Not long the hapleſs youth had wept
  Beneath the beeches ſhade,
Ere oft-repeated ſhricks he heard
  Re-echo through the glade.

Sunk as he was in bitter woe,
  Yet ftill his generous heart
Was ready, when diftrefs implor'd,
  Its fuccour to impart.

Inftant he rufhes to the path
  That opens through the wood;
Ah! what a fpe&acle of woe
  His eyes that inftant view'd!

A fiery courfer from her feat
  A lady gay had thrown;
Who hanging by the tender foot,
  He dragg'd remorfelefs on.

And while he furious drove between
  The thick furrounding wood,
Her pallid face, and flowing hair,
  Were all imbru'd with blood.

A fight fo fad the hardeft heart
  Had fure to pity turn'd;
What then did *Edwy*'s feel, which ftill
  Had with the mourner mourn'd?

As quick as thought he crofs'd and check'd
  The wild impetuous fteed,
And from her dreadful bondage foon
  The hopelefs lady freed.

But fure th'emotions of his foul
  No language can exprefs,
When all *Edilda*'s charms appear'd
  Upon the fair-one's face!

Nor lefs did her aftonifh'd heart
  With pow'rful feelings beat,
When in a goatherd's garb fhe faw
  Young *Edwy* at her feet.

Upon his breaft her lovely head
  He laid with tender care,
And trembling wip'd away the blood
  That foil'd her face and hair:

And while he wip'd the clotted gore,
  Almoft expir'd with fear!
Left underneath fome deadly gafh
  Should fuddenly appear.

But though full many a ruthlefs bruife
  And bleeding fcratch he found;
His heart was comforted to learn
  There was no mortal wound.

With fweet confufion, fear, and love,
  The blufhing Beauty lay,
And feem'd on *Edwy's* panting breaft
  To figh her foul away.

And while he gently footh'd her foul,
  " O! would to God," fhe faid,
" That *Edwy* was of noble birth,
  " Or I fome lowly maid!

" O! would to God this throbbing heart
  " Its gratitude could prove,
" And fhow it values not the world
  " Compar'd with *Edwy's* love!"

Juſt as the words eſcap'd her lips,
  From out a thicket by,
The haughty *Edbald* fiercely ruſh'd
  With peril in his eye.

" Die, baſe-born ſlave !" he ſcornful cry'd,
  " Who dar'ſt exalt thine eyes
" To what the monarchs of the earth
  " Might deem a noble prize !"

Then at the Youth, ſurpris'd, unarm'd,
  His ſpear he baſely puſh'd ;
But miſs'd his aim, while on his throat
  The nimble *Edwy* ruſh'd.

Quick with a ſtrenuous griping hand
  He wrench'd the ſpear away,
Then ſpurn'd him back, and at his feet
  The furious *Edbald* lay.

And while with ſcorn above his head
  He ſhook the glittering ſpear ;
" Proud Lord," he cried, " my arm ere this
  " Has laid thee proſtrate there.

" Nay, as a voucher for the deed,
  " Behold this valued ſword !
" So ſhall not mine, like thine, appear
  " An empty vaunter's word."

But now *Edilda*'s piercing ſhricks
  Had echoed through the wood,
And met her noble Father's ear,
  Who faſt the ſounds purſu'd.

Fast he the thrilling founds purfu'd
    With anguifh in his breaft,
For by her cries he knew the maid
    Full forely was diftrefs'd.

But who can fpeak his vaft furprife,
    When groveling on the ground,
Beneath a lowly goatherd's feet,
    The fiery Earl he found?

Who can his wonder fpeak, when now,
    Beneath the rough difguife,
The much-lov'd *Edwy*'s well-known face
    Appears before his eyes?

To meet his fteps with timid look
    The blufhing Shepherd came;
Nor was that blufh the offspring bafe
    Of trembling guilt or fhame.

For well he wote a heavy charge
    Earl *Edbald* would prepare,
With vengeance fill'd, and jealous hate,
    To win the Warrior's ear.

And who not kens that virtuous minds
    Awake to noble fame,
Prize far before this fpark of life
    A bright and fpotlefs name?

But lo! before his lips could ope,
    His foe impatient cries;
" If *Galvan* cares for *Edbald*'s love,
    " That fpecious villain dies.

" Here, underneath the fecret fhade,
　" Upon his bafe-born breaft,
" I faw that cold, that fcornful Maid,
　" Her head impaffion'd reft.

" Who but muft know this dark difguife
　" Was for the purpofe made?
" Who but muft know for this fhe fled
　" With art to feek the fhade?

" And whilft her foft deceitful tongue
　" Its tender love exprefs'd,
" The villain faw, and aim'd a fword,
　" Infidious, at my breaft.

" Aftonifh'd at a fcene fo ftrange,
　" A vantage great he found,
" And laid me with a fudden blow
　" Unwarn'd upon the ground.

" Nay, had not in a lucky hour
　" The noble *Galvan* came,
" His fword had buried in my breaft
　" At once their love and fhame."

More had he faid, but that his fpeech,
　With quick indignant eye,
With burning cheek, and mingled air
　Of fcorn and dignity,

The fair *Edilda* fudden here
　With interruption crofs'd:
" Bafe man!" fhe cried, " to truth, to fhame,
　" To honour, wholly loft.

" As far above thy calumny
  " Shall *Edwy*'s virtues fhine,
" As his pure foul fuperior is
  " To fuch a foul as thine.

" Thus wrong'd, deceit and dread I fcorn;
  " Then let my Father's ear,
" Let all the world in witnefs ftand;
  " To what I loud declare:

" Yes, long I've lov'd this gallant Youth,
  " And ftill his heart fhall be
" Above the greateft monarch's vows,
  " Cherifh'd and priz'd by me.

" Yet never till the morn foregone
  " The love within her breaft,
" Conceal'd with care, *Edilda*'s tongue
  " To *Edwy*'s heart confefs'd.

" Nor then the virtuous youth had kenn'd
  " The dart that rankled there,
" Had not unthought-of chance betray'd
  " The fecret to his ear.

" Yet fancy not *Edilda*'s foul,
  " By paffion blindly fway'd,
" A daughter's duty to her love
  " The facrifice has made.

" No fooner were her thoughts reveal'd,
  " Than fhe refolv'd to prove
" The bitt'reft forrows that could flow
  " From difappointed love.

" For *Galvan's* fame, and noble blood,
  " I fwear fhall never be,
" Whatever mifery is my doom,
  " Difhonour'd firft in me.

" Nor did the generous *Edwy* ftrive
  " To win with guile my heart;
" Nor breathe one wifh *Edilda's* foul
  " From duty fhould depart.

" Hence in difguife this morn he left
  " His favour, fortunes, fame;
" Grateful and virtuous, freely hence
  " An outcaft he became.

" Hence hap'ly wand'ring through this wood,
  " He faw my wretched meed;
" And hence to fave my threaten'd life
  " Flew with an angel's fpeed.

" Witnefs thefe bruifes and this blood
  " That ftill my bofom ftain;
" Nay, witnefs thou ignoble Lord,
  " Bafe author of my pain.

" And well thou know'ft the gentle youth
  " Sought not the mortal ftrife;
" Know'ft well, he baffled thy bafe arm,
  " But to preferve his life.

" But in her Father's prefence now
  " His injur'd daughter fwears
" (And well he knows her dauntlefs foul
  " His truth and firmnefs bears),

" That fooner fhall the cruel hawk
  " Mate with the gentle dove,
" Than e'er this bofom fhall incline
  " To favour *Edbald*'s love.

" In this alone a father's will,
  " His force, nay *tears*, I'll brave,
" *Edilda*'s proftituted vows
  " No hufband e'er fhall have."

The generous Beauty ended here;
  And on her ardent tongue
Her Father's ear with wonder, grief,
  And deep attention, hung.

He knew her noble nature well,
  And well her honour knew;
Nor doubted once the candid tale
  Her lips had fpoke was true.

To *Edwy* now he frowning turn'd,
  And with a fmother'd figh
Afk'd " What to *Edbald*'s heavy charge
  " He juftly could reply?"

" Thy gracious Daughter," he return'd,
  " For *Edwy* hath reply'd,
" With truth her lips the charge againft
  " His honour have deny'd.

" If to have lov'd her be a crime;
  " Or if to love her ftill
" While life remains, a crime can be,
  " Your vengeance now fulfil.

" And while my weary life you take,
  " From length of mifery,
" Believe, my Lord, your bounteous hand
  " Will only fet me free.

" Yet this my outrag'd honour afks,
  " From noble *Ofred*'s hand,
" Let my good Lord, when I am dead,
  " A few fad lines demand.

" Thofe few fad lines my pen alone
  " To *Galvan*'s eye addrefs'd,
" And thofe, without difguife, will fhow
  " The purpofe of my breaft."

" Whate'er thy guilt," the Noble cried,
  " Forbid it, gracious Heaven!
" This thanklefs hand fhould fpill his blood,
  " By whom my life was given.

" Yet on thy peril from my court
  " For ever far remove;
" Nor let thy foul dare lift a thought
  " To fuch unequal love.

" But griev'd is *Galvan* to pronounce,
  " That noble *Edbald*'s heart
" Muft now, by adverfe fate impell'd,
  " From what it wifh'd depart.

" *Galvan* nor doubts but *Edbald*'s tongue
  " The thought within his breaft,
" By outward circumftance mifled,
  " Sincerely hath exprefs'd.
                    Y

" But fince *Edilda's* heart has ftoop'd
  " To prize a vaffal's vows;
" And nought but flight and bitter hate
  " On worthy love beftows;

" Let high-born *Edbald's* better thoughts
  " Her worthlefs beauties fcorn;
" And quick to heal his wounded peace
  " To *Egbert's* court return."

The haughty Earl no anfwer gave,
  With rage his bofom burn'd,
With fullen fhame and vengeance, while
  With *Galvan* he return'd.

With noble *Galvan* he return'd,
  And with *Edilda* fair,
Silent and fad : and at the hall,
  When all alighted were,

Each to a feveral chamber went,
  To ponder o'er alone
The various chances which the peace
  Of each had overthrown.

Yet not a heart in *Galvan's* court
  But *Edwy's* fortunes mourn'd ;
Nor was there one but griev'd to fee
  His haughty foe return'd.

And much they pray'd fome ftroke of fate
  Might ftill propitious prove,
To crown the fweet *Edilda's* wifh,
  And profper *Edwy's* love.

EDWY AND EDILDA.

PART IV

BUT *Edwy*, who at *Galvan*'s word
  Submiffive left the wood,
Meantime to ancient *Hilda*'s farm
  The well-known path purfu'd.

The well-known path his feet purfu'd;
  Not fo his tortur'd mind,
Whofe every thought intently dwelt
  On what was left behind.

Ere long at *Hilda*'s door he ftands;
  And while his rough difguife,
His haggard looks, and alter'd mien,
  Conceal'd him from all eyes;

Of *Hilda*'s Hind he humbly afks
  If that her dwelling were;
And feigns from *Edwy* to be charg'd
  With fomething for her ear.

" If aught to *Hilda* thou would'ft fay,
  " It quickly muft be faid,"
The Hind return'd; " for fhe will foon
  " Be number'd with the dead.

" Struck fudden by the hand of death,
  " She prays but to furvive
" Till gallant *Edwy* from the court
  " Of *Galvan* fhall arrive.

" Nor is an hour elaps'd, or ere
  " A meffenger in hafte
" She fent, to beg his prefence here
  " Before fhe breath'd her laft."

" Lead me, O lead me to her bed !"
  The feeming goatherd cries ;
While to conceal the burfting woe,
  He muffles up his eyes.

To *Hilda*'s couch he led him ftraight,
  And at his earneft pray'r
Before his errand was reveal'd
  Retir'd and left him there.

Then while his ftreaming eyes he ftill
  With his fpread hand did fhroud;
And kneeling by the bed of death
  His anguifh fobb'd aloud :

The dying *Hilda* turn'd her eye,
  And feeing him, did crave,
With feeble voice, " What brought him there
  " And what with her he'd have ?"

" O ! 'tis your *Edwy*, your dear fon,"
  He movingly replies,
" Who in a heavy hour is come
  " To clofe a parent's eyes."

Then her cold hand, bedew'd by death,
  He foftly, kindly preft ;
Kifs'd her pale lips, and laid her head
  Gently upon his breaft.

" Welcome, thou joy of *Hilda*'s foul !
  " Thrice welcome art thou here !
" But wherefore in a garb fo mean
  " Doth *Edwy* now appear ?

" And wherefore have his haggard cheeks,"
  She cried, " forgot their bloom ?
" Ah ! why this fpectacle of woe
  " Doth *Edwy* hither come ?"

" Let not my honour'd parent feek,"
  The youth return'd, " to know
" What to the pains of this fick couch
  " Would add a load of woe.

" O ! rather be it *Edwy*'s part
  " To catch her dying breath ;
" And with his filial tendernefs
  " To fmooth the bed of death."

" Ev'n as thou wilt," fhe low reply'd,
  " And well it doth appear
" Not to confume in fruitlefs talk
  " My little remnant here.

" Since ere my ebbing life is gone,
  " Fain would I have it known
" To *Edwy*'s heart, that *Hilda* ne'er
  " In *Edwy* had a fon.

" Nay, ftart not thus, nor break my tale,
　" But calmly hear the reft,
" Which long in fecret hath repos'd
　" In *Hilda's* cautious breaft.

" Full twenty years are paft and gone
　" Since to the bloody fray
" *Ongar,* in aid of *Egbert's* arms,
　" From *Hilda* hied away.

" Hied far away to Cornwall's coafts,
　" What time the barb'rous Dane
" Frighted her peace, and fertile fields
　" With native blood did ftain.

" It happen'd from thofe horrid fcenes,
　" As through a fhady wood,
" *Ongar* to feek our lowly home
　" One morn his way purfu'd ;

" Within its moft fecluded paths,
　" A dying wretch he found,
" Gafh'd o'er with wounds, and in his gore
　" All welt'ring on the ground.

" Already did his pallid face,
　" Death's ghaftly femblance bear ;
" And by a few convulfive ftarts
　" Life only glimmer'd there.

" Yet, ah ! the moving fight to fee,
　" Clofe to his bloody breaft,
" Ev'n in the agonies of death,
　" His arms an infant preft.

" Shock'd at the fcene, my hufband haftes
  " His fuccour to impart;
" And gently lifts the dying wretch,
  " And gently chafes his heart.

" One little flafh of life returns:
  " He lifts his languid eyes,
" And thus, with lab'ring catching breath,
  " In feeble accents cries:

" *Regard not me!—fave the dear child!*
  " *For*—more he would have faid,
" But life, exhaufted in th' attempt,
  " A paufe eternal made.

" And let *me* hafte, while breath remains,
  " To clofe the piteous tale;
" Left death in everlafting bonds,
  " My tongue, like his, fhould feal.

" The lovely infant *Ongar* took
  " From its dead father's fide,
" And tendful of his little charge,
  " To *Hilda*'s dwelling hy'd.

" Moft welcome he to *Hilda*'s arms
  " With the fweet babe return'd;
" Who a dear infant's recent death
  " Inceffantly had mourn'd.

" And while he told its early woes,
  " I wept, and to my breaft,
" With all a mother's yearnings, clofe
  " The fmiling orphan prefs'd.

" Ev'n from that hour my heart for thee,
 " A mother's fondeft love,
" Her tender fears, and anxious cares,
 " Hath never ceas'd to prove.

" And from thy kind, thy virtuous heart,
 " Hath *Hilda* ever known
" All the obedience, love, and care,
 " Of the moft tender fon!

" But what thy haplefs father's name,
 " Or what his birth and ftate,
" In vain to *Edwy*'s longing ear
 " Would *Hilda*'s tongue relate.

" Too foon again to Cornwall's coafts
 " Fell war my hufband bore,
" And there my fofter infant's birth
 " He promis'd to explore.

" But ah! no more thefe eyes beheld,
 " No more thefe arms embrac'd
" The man they lov'd! in prime of life
 " Ordain'd to breathe his laft.

" Nor had my tongue from *Edwy*'s ear
 " So long the tale conceal'd,
" If aught to blefs, or footh his heart,
 " That tongue could have reveal'd.

" And yet perhaps thefe lips ere now
 " Had told the piteous tale,
" And from unconfcious *Edwy*'s eyes
 " Remov'd the fecret veil;

" Had not I fondly fear'd thy love
" For *Hilda* might decay ;
" Or that thy steps, to trace thy birth,
" Might wander far away.

" And oh! forgive, thou generous youth,
" If doating *Hilda*'s heart,
" Her husband lost, from all it lov'd,
" In *Edwy* fear'd to part.

" Yet though thy robe with clotted gore
" And dirt was all besprent,
" And had by some uncourteous hand
" Been quite asunder rent ;

" This did the substance still declare,
" That, nor of abject race,
" Nor yet of scanty pen'ry's stock,
" My darling *Edwy* was.

" And round thy little wrist was bound
" A curious braid of hair,
" Which by a heart of precious stone
" Was firmly fasten'd there.

" But when too big for such a band,
" Thy growing wrist became,
" I safe preserv'd this only pledge
" Of *Edwy*'s birth or name.

" O! may it prove in *Edwy*'s hand
" A great auspicious light,
" To chase away the envious cloud
" That hangs before his sight!

" O ! may the gracious Pow'r above
" Direct his goings ſtill,
" Lead him to every earthly good,
" And keep him far from ill!"

She could no more ; for Death's cold damps
Upon her forehead hung,
Within her filmy eye he glar'd,
And mutter'd on her tongue.

Yet ſtill upon her *Edwy*'s face,
While any ſenſe remain'd,
She fondly gaz'd ; and ſtill his hand
With chilly graſp retain'd.

Still did his tears and ſoothings ſoft
The pangs of death beguile ;
And as he pour'd his grateful thanks
For all her cares, a ſmile

'Through the dread ſhadowings of death
Once more did faintly break ;
And when the ſtruggling ſpirit fled,'
Yet loiter'd on her cheek.

To her remains the grateful youth
The laſt ſad duties paid,
And water'd with his tears the turf
That o'er her corſe was laid :

Then from the ſcenes of former peace,
Determin'd far to ſtray,
And in ſome deep ſequeſter'd ſhade
Weep all his life away.

" What has an outcaft like myfelf,"
  He cried, " to do with men,
" Whofe int'refts and connexions make
  " This world a cheerful fcene ?

" But *Edwy* from the ties of blood
  " Cut off for ever here,
" To intereft dead, a fingle wretch
  " Muft on the earth appear.

" No dear connexions, tender ties,
  " In life he e'er can have ;
" And from his woes can only reft
  " Within the filent grave.

" Then let the wretched orphan hafte,
  " To hide his abject head ;
" Loft and forgotten by the world
  " In fome fecluded fhade!

" Yet ftill amidft retirement's gloom,
  " For fweet *Edilda*'s peace
" This tongue fhall pray, and afk from Heav'n
  " No bleffing but her blifs.

" And like a radiant angel ftill
  " Her image fhall appear,
" Tinted by love's own hand, to charm
  " The horrors of defpair."

With foft laments, and yearnings fond,
  Thus *Edwy* onward paft;
And many a long and weary mile
  With wand'ring footfteps trac'd;

Throughout the day his journey ſtill
   By private paths purſu'd;
And laid his weary limbs at night
   Within ſome gloomy wood.

His weary limbs at reſt he laid;
   But rarely to his heart,
Awake with woe, could balmy ſleep
   His needful aid impart.

Three tedious days and watchful nights
   The haplefs *Edwy* ſped;
Yet kenn'd not the defir'd retreat
   Wherein to hide his head.

The fourth his feet a foreſt trod
   What time the ſhades of night,
Juſt fall'n, were ſweetly awful made
   By Luna's ſober light.

Within the deep and ancient ſhade
   As ſlow he onward wends,
The ſilver regent journeying bright,
   A gleam to guide him ſends.

And through the branches, as by breaks,
   Her rays ſerenely ſhine,
To the majeſtic wood they give
   Solemnity divine!

All Nature ſeem'd in ſilence huſh'd,
   Save where the plaintive ſong
Of *Philomel,* to hail the moon,
   Was heard the woods among.

The mournful lay, as on he paſt,
　Sunk deep in *Edwy*'s ſoul ;
And for a moment from his griefs
　His rapt attention ſtole.

But quickly with redoubled force
　His bitter ſorrows flow :
" Ah ! fancy not," he cried, " thy ſong
　" Pre-eminent in woe !

" If *Edwy*'s notes to *Edwy*'s heart
　" Their accents but incline ;
" Thou'lt own, ſweet bird, thy plaintive tale
　" A jocund ſtrain to mine."

He ſaid ; and ſitting on a ſtone,
　So ſad, ſo ſweet, did play,
That *Philomela*, charm'd to hear,
　Forgot her humbler lay.

As *Orpheus* fabled was of old,
　The tufted groves among,
To ſit and charm the ſilent ſhades
　With his melodious ſong ;

So *Edwy* breath'd his melting tones
　On the ſtill ear of night ;
Whoſe calmneſs wafted through the wood
　Each note, with ſtrange delight !

Till ſo reſponſive to his woe
　He touch'd the mournful lay,
That melting on his own ſad ſtrain,
　His ſpirits dy'd away.

B b

From his faint hand the tuneful pipe
   Infenfibly did part,
While heavy languor clos'd his eyes,
   And ficken'd round his heart.

Nor came the tranced fpirits back,
   Till gentle on his breaft
A hand he felt, while thus a voice
   Benign his ear addrefs'd :

" If fenfe be with the life return'd,
   " That beats within thy heart,
" Look up, fad youth, and to a friend
   " Thy miferies impart.

" For well this bofom is attun'd
   " To forrow's plaintive tone ;
" And how to footh another's woe
   " Is tutor'd by its own."

He faid, and figh'd.   The tender words
   Touch'd *Edwy's* inmoft foul;
While wonder at the ftrange addrefs,
   And awe, his mind control.

As to fome haplefs wretch new wak'd,
   Ev'n yet the pleafing dream,
Juft fled, he knows not, or as truth
   Or fiction to efteem ;

So *Edwy's* fenfes fcarce return'd,
   Confefs'd a fecret fear,
Left the fweet founds were fancy all
   That feem'd to greet his ear.

But doubt a certainty became,
  And rev'rence and furprife
His bofom fill, as lifting now
  His newly open'd eyes,

By the pale moon's foft ftreaming light,
  That quiver'd through the wood,
A holy Hermit at his fide
  The love-lorn Shepherd view'd.

A fable mantle flowing large,
  The reverend figure clad,
On which his long and filver beard
  With every motion play'd.

As fome bright meteor graceful hangs
  Upon the veil of night,
So flow'd the waving ringlets down
  With fulleft honours dight.

Nor were the honours of his head
  Inferior yet, I ween,
Whofe plenteous locks full many a day
  Had, by their whitenefs, feen.

A fpirit in his fpeaking eye
  Chaften'd by forrow fat;
And human kindnefs, fenfe, and truth,
  Right fairly fhow'd thereat.

His fhape and height were of the beft,
  And in his graceful mien
A reference fair to better days,
  And happier hours, was feen.

A dignity devoid of pride
　　Sat full upon his brow;
And, fpite of time, his comely age
　　A lovely youth did fhow.

Yet comelier had his years appear'd,
　　And on his reverend face
The furrows lefs, had pining grief
　　Not deepen'd age's trace.

His eye, with mingled awe and love,
　　Admiring *Edwy* hung
Upon the Sage, while mildly thus
　　Rejoin'd his graceful tongue:

" Whence art thou come, thou youth forlorn,
　" Who this fequefter'd fhade,
" At night's ftill hour, haft with thy pipe
　" So fweetly vocal made?

" But thou art faint, thy fpirits much
　" By wearinefs opprefs'd,
" And bitter woe, require the aid
　" Of food and balmy reft.

" To *Herman*'s cave thy feeble fteps
　" His foftering arm fhall lead;
" And there thy wearied limbs fhall reft
　" Upon his humble bed.

" He doubts not but his tender care
　" Sweet folace may impart;
" Nor yet defpairs, with counfel fweet
　" To eafe thy lab'ring heart.

" For fure the verieft wretch muft find
 " Some fymptoms of relief,
" To own a friend who knows to feel,
 " And loves to fhare his grief.

" Too well thy eye and haggard cheek
 " Confefs corroding care;
" And yet believe, his keener touch
 " Thefe deep-worn furrows bear."

" Ah, no!" the fighing youth return'd
 With warmth, " there cannot be
" Throughout the earth a wretch involv'd
 " In deeper woe than me.

" Yet, honour'd Sage, if aught on earth
 " Can foften *Edwy*'s grief,
" From thy fweet counfel he may hope
 " To gather fome relief.

" Thy generous kindnefs he accepts;
 " And *Herman* ne'er fhall find
" That generous kindnefs thrown away
 " Upon a thanklefs mind.

" Yet what have I but pray'rs, and love,
 " And gratitude, to give?
" And what befides would *Herman* deign
 " From *Edwy* to receive?

" Nor fhall the fortunes of my life
 " Be hidden from thine ear,
" If I have pow'r to tell the tale,
 " And patience thou to hear."

He faid: the while to *Herman*'s cave
    Their focial fteps were bent;
And ftill on his fupporting arm
    The feeble *Edwy* leant.

And ftill the Sage, with foothing words,
    Spoke comfort to his heart;
Still to revive his drooping fprite,
    Exerted every art.

Not long their friendly fteps had trod
    The mazes of the wood,
Or e'er, by Luna's trembling light,
    The welcome cave they view'd.

Deep in a private dale that funk
    The towering woods between,
Scoop'd from a high and craggy cliff,
    The lone abode was feen.

Nor yet unlovely was the rock,
    Whofe rugged fides were made
Gracefully gloomy, by a foft
    Variety of fhade.

From out its clefts the berried afh,
    And flow'ring hawthorn grew;
And there the trembling poplar's fhade
    Mix'd with the mournful yew.

And as their branches interwove,
    Now here, now there, was feen
A moffy crag, that thruft its point
    The motley fhade between.

Full in the bofom of the rock
   A cryftal riv'let fprung,
And dafhing down from clift to clift
   Its white foam fcattering flung.

By breaks the branches bow'ring o'er,
   Conceal'd it from the eye,
Except that through the leaves, by peeps,
   Its glimmerings one might fpy.

The whole a fhade more copious crown'd,
   And proudly o'er the reft
An aged oak, with branches wild,
   Exalted high its creft.

A gloomy yew of ancient date
   That ftood before the cave,
With ample honours to the fcene
   An added beauty gave.

Around its trunk a ruftic feat
   Above the turf was rear'd;
And at its foot the murm'ring brook
   With fhining face appeard.

The fhelvings of the fecret dale
   With wood of various green
Were cover'd thick, fave where a rock,
   Or flanting field, was feen.

Yet narrow were the fields I trow,
   And little had to fpare
For the white fheep that o'er their face
   Sparingly fprinkled were.

Upon the heights the lofty wood
  With gloomy honours wav'd;
And ftill from every nipping blaft
  The fhelter'd valley fav'd.

Charm'd with the calm romantic fcene,
  Which yet more pleafing fhow'd
As Luna filver'd all the dale,
  While riding o'er the wood;

The Youth exclaim'd, " How pleas'd could I,
  " Within this private dale,
" With honour'd *Herman*'s converfe fweet,
  " And meditation, dwell!"

" And here *fhall* dwell," the Sage reply'd,
  " If fo thy foul incline;
" And here well pleas'd will *Herman* be
  " To mix his tears with thine:

" Well pleas'd will be, thou gentle youth,
  " To liften to thy lays;
" And court thy hand to clofe his eyes
  " When death fhall end his days.

" For kindred *Edwy*'s forrows feem,
  " Kindred his foul to mine;
" And through his griefs the genuine fparks
  " Of heav'n-born virtue fhine.

" Here, firm united by the bands
  " Of friendfhip, we will dwell;
" And think with fcorn upon a world
  " Fond mortals love fo well.

" Nor vice, nor pride, nor difcontent,
  " Shall in this cell appear;
" But peace, and piety, and love,
  " Shall fweetly flourifh here.

" Then enter in, a welcome gueft;
  " And while thy lips difclofe
" Thy fad mifhaps, my heart fhall feel,
  " And, feeling, footh thy woes."

He faid; and enter'd with the youth,
  Whofe weary drooping head
His hands benevolent repos'd
  Upon the moffy bed.

And now with milk, and various fruits,
  The table he prepares;
And *Edwy*'s deep-dejected mind
  With wholefome nurture cheers.

His ftrength recruited, foon the youth
  Begins his tale of woe;
And fhows, impartial, every caufe,
  From whence his forrows flow.

Sincerely fhows his inmoft heart;
  The while upon his tongue,
The Sage with tender fympathy,
  And deep attention, hung.

But when to *Hilda*'s bed of death,
  He brings the mournful tale;
While he relates her dying fpeech,
  The Sage's cheek grows pale.

D d

Paler and paler now it grows;
    The while his heaving breaft,
His trembling lip, and eager eye,
    The lab'ring foul confeft.

The youth with dread obferv'd the change,
    And made a fudden paufe;
Then tenderly of *Herman*'s ill
    Inquires the latent caufe.

" Afk not," he cries, " what roufes thus
    " A tempeft in my breaft;
" Purfue thy tale, my bofom throbs,
    " Nay burns, to know the reft!"

Amaz'd! the youth his tale purfu'd;
    But when, to prove his birth,
He nam'd the bracelet, as his pledge,
    His *only* pledge on earth;

" Show me that pledge!" the Sage exclaim'd!
    And when the pledge *was* fhown,
Upon his neck he fell, and cry'd,
    " Thou art! thou *art* my fon!"

" How! whence! where!"—wild, the youth
    " Sure it can never be,   [exclaims,
" That haplefs *Edwy* fhould poffefs
    " A father fuch as thee!"

Yet while he doubted, trembled, wept,
    The Hermit he carefs'd;
Who clafp'd him clofe in fpeechlefs joy
    Unto his aged breaft.

" O ! doubt it not, dear youth," he cry'd,
　" Thou art indeed my Son ;
" Nor yet a Father, fuch as me,
　" Shall *Edwy* blufh to own."

Then more compos'd he fat, and wip'd
　The rapturous tears that fell ;
While thus to the aftonifh'd youth
　His lips began their tale :

" Well may'ft thou wonder," deareft youth,
　" At what a Father fpoke,
" When too intemp'rate from his lips,
　" The heat-felt tranfports broke.

" But who, inur'd to long diftrefs,
　" And long from hope confin'd,
" Can feel the fudden burft of joy,
　" And curb his ftruggling mind ?

" Yet long as forrow on my foul
　" Its bitternefs hath prefs'd,
" My greateft joy will be to chafe
　" Affliction from thy breaft.

" Nay, weep not thus, nor look aghaft,
　" For forrow now is o'er;
" But liften while my lips unfold
　" A thoufand joys in ftore :

" A thoufand joys, which all a dream
　" Had feem'd the hour foregone;
" But which thy panting heart fhall foon
　" Sincere and poignant own.

" Know then, thou comfort of my foul,
   " That *Galvan*'s felf to thee,
" In point of wealth, muft yield the palm,
   " And noble anceftry.

" Tho' chang'd my name, yet know thy birth
   " From far-fam'd *Ofwald* fprung;
" Whofe great defcent, and pow'r as great,
   " Was heard from every tongue.

" Superior yet thy birth appears
   " Upon thy Mother's fide,
" Who near to *Brithric*'s royal blood,
   " And *Egbert*'s, was ally'd.

" But what avail'd my *Thyra*'s blood!
   " And what her virtues all!
" Ordain'd by barb'rous ruffians hands,
   " In beauty's bloom to fall!

" Yet ftill her well-remember'd charms
   " Upon my *Edwy*'s face,
" And ftill her manners fweet in thine,
   " A father's eye can trace.

" Nine years a heav'n within her arms,
   " Did happy *Ofwald* prove;
" And five fweet infants did fhe bring
   " As pledges of his love.

" But at one deadly fweep, the lofs
   " Of all, thy father mourn'd;
" Though now in fuch a fon as thee,
   " They all appear return'd.

" A caftle fair on *Devon*'s edge,
  " Thy father lov'd full well ;
" And there, withdrawn from bufier fcenes,
  " At times, was wont to dwell.

" Thither my lovely Wife retir'd,
  " What time, full many a Dane,
" Invading Cornwall's further fide,
  " By *Egbert*'s arms were flain.

" Thefe robbers quell'd, I eager fought
  " The fcenes of former peace ;
" Sought the fair meed of all my toils
  " In fweet domeftic blifs.

" But ah ! too foon the heart of man,
  " To confidence a prey,
" At fortune's firft delufive finile,
  " Cafts prudent care away.

" Thus *Ofwald* fearlefsly repos'd
  " Upon his *Thyra*'s breaft,
" Nor dreamt of any rifing ftorm
  " To ruffle his calm reft.

" One night awak'd from balmy fleep
  " Within her faithful arms,
" A horrid clamour inftant fill'd
  " My heart with ftrange alarms.

" Rufhing from off my downy couch,
  " Quick to the hall I paft,
" Where trufty *Algar* met my fteps,
  " With wild diforder'd hafte.

E e

" His arm my little *Ofbert* bore;
    " And as my way he croft,
' Fly quick! my Lord,' he trembling cry'd,
    ' Fly quick! or all is loft!

' The cruel Danes impetuous rufh
    ' Upon thy guardian train;
' And ere I ran to fave thy fon,
    ' But few were left unflain.

' The remnant doubtlefs of that force,
    ' Which late in Cornwall's field,
' The royal *Egbert*'s gallant troops
    ' So bravely met and quell'd.

' Thence flying, they've furpris'd thy train
    ' Beneath the mafk of night:
' But urge thy fpeed!   A moment hence
    ' May be too late for flight.'

" He fpake, and vanifh'd from my eyes :—
    " Fell anguifh rent my breaft;
" Yet to my *Thyra* back with fpeed
    " My eager footfteps preft;

" Refolv'd on danger's utmoft brink,
    " Whatever might betide,
" To fave her life, or lofe my own,
    " With honour, by her fide.

" But ah! before my fteps return'd,
    " The clamour caught her ear;
" And by a different way, too foon!
    " She fled, o'erwhelm'd with fear.

" Diftracted I return once more
" Unto the empty hall,
" And there, with horror compafs'd round,
" Aloud for fuccour call!

" Nor call in vain, though moft had fall'n
" To filent death a prey ;
" A few remain'd who heard my voice,
" And hurried me away.

" But not to where the bloody Danes,
" Through the long galleries pour;
" To ftop the flood, or meet his death,
" Their ftruggling Lord they bore.

" In vain I threaten'd, rav'd, and pray'd ;
" Swift from the defp'rate fight
" They bore me with a cruel care,
" Beneath the gloom of night.

" And oft, in vain! I anxious afk,
" If aught of Thyra's fate,
" Or of my children's, to my ear
" Their knowledge can relate ?

" At laft, when far from fcenes of death
" In fafety I was plac'd,
" Seeing the horrors of fufpenfe,
" My fpirits widely wafte ;

" They tell, with many a heavy groan,
" That all my daughters fair,
" And lovely Thyra, by the Danes
" Moft bafely butcher'd were.

" But ſtill of little *Oſbert*'s fate
 " No knowledge was obtain'd;
" And ſtill to ſooth my deep diſtreſs,
 " One ray of light remain'd.

" Yet, 'midſt my anguiſh, great revenge
 " Within my boſom roſe;
" And *Oſwald* ſwore he would avenge
 " His own, and Cornwall's woes.

" Soon at my wiſh a gallant troop
 " Of warriors gather'd round;
" And ſoon thoſe ſpoilers of my peace,
 " The cruel Danes, we found.

" Upon their force my warriors ruſh'd
 " Impetuous as a flood;
" And *Oſwald*'s wrongs were deep repaid
 " In their inhuman blood.

" But ſtill afflićtion pierc'd my ſoul;
 " And, like the ſtricken deer,
" Where'er I turn'd, the deadly ſhaft
 " Did in my boſom bear.

" At length, to ſum up all my woes,
 " While through this ancient wood,
" Some ſkulking Danes eſcap'd from fight,
 " My valiant train purſu'd;

" Far in the ſhade their eager feet
 " The faithful *Algar* found
" Stiff in his blood, a ghaſtly fight !
 " And gaſh'd with many a wound.

" In his clench'd hand a remnant ftill,
  " Though all with gore defil'd,
" He grafp'd, of the remember'd robe
  " That clad my darling child.

" But vainly had their faithful feet
  " Explor'd the utmoft round
" Of the vaft wood, no further trace
  " Of *Ofbert* could be found.

" The heavy tidings to my ear
  " Reluctantly they tell;
" And with thofe tidings, from my breaft
  " Each gleam of hope repel.

" For who could doubt my haplefs child
  " Kill'd by the favage Dane,
" Though his dear relics, through the wood,
  " Their care had fought in vain ?

" Sick of the world, where all my peace
  " Was at one fatal blow
" Dafh'd quite away, and nothing left
  " But unremitting woe;

" For ever from the haunts of men,
  " My foul refolv'd to ftray;
" And loft in folitude's deep gloom,
  " Weep weary life away.

" Yet think not 'midft my bitt'reft pangs
  " One doubt within my breaft,
" One impious murmur, boldly rofe
  " To combat Heav'n's beheft.

F f

" I knew the wifdom of my God,
　" His mercy knew as well;
" And judg'd, to roufe me from my fins,
　" This weight of forrow fell.

" And well religion's lore had taught,
　" Not in a world like this
" The heart of man fhould fondly reft
　" Its hope of lafting blifs.

" Submiffive, patient, and refign'd,
　" I therefore kifs'd the rod;
" And by a deep repentance fought
　" To reconcile my God.

" Unto my noble brother now
　" A meffenger I fent,
" And only to his faithful ear
　" Difclos'd my fix'd intent.

" In vain his love and friendfhip ftrove
　" To footh my tortur'd heart;
" In vain, from a refolve fo ftrange,
　" Intreated me to part.

" My vaft eftate, and honours fair,
　" I trufted to his hand;
" And only crav'd fuch fmall fupplies
　" As nature fhould demand.

" Then privately with him I fought,
　" In this deep foreft's fhade,
" A fecret place, wherein to lay
　" With folitude my head.

" For here I ween'd, in thy dear blood
  " Was feal'd my deep defpair;
" And therefore ftealing from the world,
  " Defir'd to languifh here.

" Lo! to my wifh, funk far in gloom,
  " We found this calm retreat,
" Which every thing confpir'd to make
  " For woe a dwelling meet.

" Full twenty years are paft and gone,
  " Since firft his forrows made
" Thy wretched father's heavy heart
  " Acquainted with this fhade.

" Loft to the world, full twenty years
  " In folitude I've fpent,
" Save that at times thy uncle's fteps
  " Have hitherward been bent.

" By him in fecret ftill fupply'd
  " My little ftores have been,
" His hand the fcatter'd flock beftow'd,
  " That feed the copfe between.

" And ftill his loving lips have ftrove,
  " Yet ftill have ftrove in vain,
" To win me from this lonely cave,
  " Unto the world again.

" How little did I ween that world
  " So hated, e'er would be
" Again an interefting fcene,
  " And full of joys for me!

" But far above our mortal ken
  " Is Heav'n's almighty pow'r;
" And ours is only to fubmit,
  " To feel, and to adore.

" It chanc'd as at the fall of night
  " Attentively I ſtood,
" Obſervant of the ſilver moon
  " That glimmer'd through the wood:

" Juſt at my feet ſhe brightly glanc'd
  " With clear unuſual light,
" And ſomething, ſudden, caught her rays,
  " And ſparkled to my ſight.

" I curious ſtoop'd to learn the caufe;
  " But what was my furprife,
" When this well-noted pledge of love
  " Appear'd before my eyes?

" When thy dear mother, to my wiſh,
  " Produc'd a lovely ſon,
" T' inherit *Oſwald*'s honours, wealth,
  " And blood of high renown;

" O'erjoy'd, to deck each little wriſt
  " A curious braid of hair
" Her fingers wove, which ruby hearts
  " Both crown'd and faſten'd there.

" One bracelet from her flaxen locks
  " Like gloſſy ſilk did ſhine;
" The other braid her partial hand
  " Would needs collect from mine.

" Upon the back of each bright heart
 " Thefe words engraven were,
" In myftic characters ; *fond Love
 " And Joy have fix'd me here.*

" The well-remember'd pledge of love
 " Unto my lips I preft ;
" The while a thoufand tender thoughts
 " O'erwhelm'd my throbbing breaft.

" Afrefh I wept my *Thyra's* fate ;
 " Afrefh I wept thy own ;
" And on the ground, with new defpair,
 " Diftracted threw me down.

" But foon thy notes, fo ftrangely fweet !
 " So mournful ! caught my ear,
" That from affliction's felf they ftole
 " A wifh to hufh and hear.

" And as I hark'd, I long'd to know
 " What mortal 'midft this fhade,
" Its deep and unfrequented gloom
 " So fweetly vocal made.

" Thou know'ft the reft ; for while I ftole
 " With filence to the found,
" It ceas'd ; and foon I faw thee ftretch'd
 " In fwoonings on the ground :

" Too happy that my feeble hand
 " Affiftance could impart,
" And bring my *Edwy* back to life,
 " To blefs his woeful heart.

" And fure this memorable night
   " My fteps were led by Heav'n;
" This bracelet furely as a pledge
   " Of coming joy was given.

" By this the anfwering pledge of love
   " More perfectly was known;
" By this thy father was prepar'd
   " To meet and know his fon.

" Nor haughty *Edbald*, proudly, now
   " His honours fhall compare,
" His large poffeffions, pow'r, or birth,
   " With *Ofwald*'s greater heir.

" For ftill the flow'r of *Egbert*'s court,
   " The kingdom *Ofwald* deem'd;
" And *Ofwald* ftill above his peers
   " By *Egbert* was efteem'd

" The lov'd companion of his youth,
   " And fharer of his fate,
" What time in foreign climes he dwelt
   " From jealous *Brithric*'s hate.

" And noble *Galvan* well I know,
   " And often he has fwore,
" That *Ofwald*'s friendfhip he efteem'd
   " All friendfhip far before.

" But now 'tis meet thy weary limbs
   " Were fteep'd in balmy reft;
" And needful is the foft repofe
   " That long has left thy breaft.

" To-morrow with the rifing fun
   " Straight to my Brother's court,
" With new-born hope, and peace, and joy,
   " Together we'll refort.

" From thence to noble *Galvan*'s hall
   " A meffenger with fpeed
" Will *Ofwald* fend, that he may learn
   " What fortune has decreed :

" What fav'ring Heav'n has rather done
   " To blefs a virtuous pair,
" Ordaining who fo lowly feem'd,
   " A pow'rful noble's heir.

" Nor fhall thy heart from her it loves
   " A longer feafon wait,
" Than *Ofwald*'s heir can be prepar'd
   " To go with fitting ftate.

" Beneath the reft at *Galvan*'s court
   " Thou hitherto haft been ;
" But now exalted o'er them all
   " My *Edwy* fhall be feen.

" By that dear name thy father flill
   " His long-loft fon muft call,
" Since under that dear name he came
   " To end his bitter thrall."

The reverend Noble ended here:
   But who the joy can tell
With which the youth's enraptur'd foul
   Did on each accent dwell ?

Who the ftrong extafies can paint
   That in his bofom glow'd ?
Who the warm tide that from his lips
   Of love and duty flow'd ?

In vain his father's tender care
   Had hop'd the balmy reft ;
A thoufand tranfports drove it far
   From *Edwy*'s panting breaft.

And oft he queftion'd his fond heart,
   And often felt a fear,
Left all illufion was the blifs
   That newly buftled there.

And oft he wifh'd to urge the hours,
   Oft figh'd for morn's return,
Impatient that *Edilda*'s heart
   His alter'd ftate might learn.

Yet fometimes heav'd a fecret figh,
   Left *Galvan*'s ftern command,
Or foft'ning tears, her heart had bow'd
   To haughty *Edbald*'s hand.

END OF THE FOURTH PART.

EDWY AND EDILDA.

PART V

BUT sweet the cares which love had blent
  With joy, in *Edwy*'s breast ;
Far other than the deadly pangs
  That broke *Edilda*'s rest.

Within her gentle bosom, hope
  Withdrew her genial ray ;
And sorrow sat triumphant there,
  And frown'd the smiles away.

Yet still amidst her deep distress,
  Her self-approving thought,
To ward the horrors of despair,
  Its lenient soothings brought.

And though she ween'd her hapless heart
  With hopeless misery strove ;
Still virtue rose with every pant,
  Though every pant was love.

Nor was her tender, generous heart,
  In noble *Galvan*'s court,
Of fickle fortune, love, and grief,
  Alone the wretched sport.

Within the haughty *Edbald*'s breaſt
  A tempeſt fiercely burn'd;
And every motion of his mind
  To wild diſtraction turn'd.

There mad'ning jealouſy and pride
  Still baffled all control;
Whilſt love affianc'd to deſpair,
  Shook, fearfully, his ſoul.

Full oft in bitterneſs of heart,
  He curs'd the fatal night,
When firſt *Edilda*'s matchleſs charms
  Beam'd, dazzling, to his ſight.

And oft the lovely maid he curſt,
  And curſt her noble Sire,
For fanning in his kindling breaſt
  Love's faſcinating fire.

But curſt his virtuous Rival moſt,
  And, fill'd with fury, ſwore,
That dreadful vengeance on his head,
  Relentleſs, he would pour.

Nay, madly ween'd, that when in duſt
  The blooming youth was laid,
Love might await the bloody hand
  That mix'd him with the dead.

Nor did his dark ſuſpicious ſoul
  Believe *Edilda*'s heart,
Spite of her vows, from what it lov'd
  So eaſily would part.

The favour'd *Edwy* ftill he deem'd
  Was lurking in the wood ;
And *there* to glut his vengeance thought
  In his detefted blood.

Four defp'rate ruffians he prepar'd,
  Ere the third day was paft ;
And bafely hop'd the fourth fhould prove
  His hated Rival's laft.

Attended by his bloody band,
  Sweet pity caft away,
He fought with execrable fpeed,
  The wood, at dawn of day.

Deluded there, he raging fearch'd
  Each humble cottage round ;
And what was *Hilda*'s farm, at laft
  With cruel tranfport found :

For there he doubted not his foul
  Its bloody will fhould have ;
And fwore, an aged mother's arms
  The victim fhould not fave :

Yet equal conflict bafely fear'd,
  And to the ruffian's knife,
Within his heart ignobly doom'd
  The blamelefs *Edwy*'s life.

But Heav'n had otherwife defign'd ;
  And jealoufy and rage,
With difappointment in his breaft,
  A mortal conteft wage.

When feeking *Edwy* from the hinds,
  Of *Hilda*'s death he heard;
And that her fon the morning paft,
  Had fudden difappear'd:

As fome gaunt wolf, fecure of prey,
  O'erleaps the neighb'ring field,
But empty finds the fence that late
  The fleecy flock had held,

So *Edbald* finds his prey efcap'd,
  And fo with tenfold rage
His bofom burns, nor aught but blood
  His fury can affuage.

Madly he roams the country round;
  But roams and raves in vain;
No tidings of the hated youth
  His keeneft fearch can gain.

Wearied at length with fruitlefs toil,
  His gloomy face he turn'd
To *Galvan*'s tow'rs; from whence, I ween,
  Not one his abfence mourn'd.

But fcarcely in the ample hall
  His fullen fteps appear,
Ere difappointment haftes afrefh
  To front and dafh him there.

For loathing ftill the vows he urg'd
  Her favour to obtain,
The fweet *Edilda* fought to fhun
  What fcorn repuls'd in vain.

Some five fhort miles from *Galvan*'s court,
  Hard by a lofty wood,
Of mickle note, and mickle ftate,
  A ponderous abbey ftood.

The abbot *Aldric* rul'd within,
  Great *Galvan*'s uncle's fon ;
For wifdom, holinefs, and pow'r,
  Throughout the kingdom known.

Oft from his lips the lovely maid
  Had drawn inftruction kind ;
And much he lov'd her generous heart,
  And much her docile mind.

And oft he vow'd, when gentle peace
  A fanctuary fair
Made her foft breaft, in happier days,
  From forrow, pain, and care ;

That if the fmiles of fortune fled,
  The honour'd maid fhould meet,
Within his abbey's hallow'd walls,
  A calm and fafe retreat.

To feek this fhelter, when the morn
  Her blufhing radiance threw
From hill-top high, and the laft fhades
  Of cowring night withdrew ;

The fweet *Edilda* filent ftole
  From *Galvan*'s portals fair ;
And long ere mid-day's fultry gleam
  Was lodg'd fecurely there.

Soon to the holy *Aldric*'s ear
   The maid difclos'd her thought;
And fhow'd the caufe why thus by ftealth
   The abbey's gloom fhe fought.

And much her virtue he admir'd,
   Her fpirit much approv'd ;
In flying the proud man fhe loath'd,
   And quitting him fhe lov'd.

Then warmly vow'd that *Edbald*'s pow'r,
   Nor *Galvan*'s ftern command,
Should aught avail, to force the maid
   From his protecting hand.

But mickle well the fair-one judg'd,
   Her Father's fecret mind
To favour haughty *Edbald*'s love
   No longer was inclin'd.

For well fhe kenn'd *that* Noble's pride,
   And paffions unfubdu'd,
His jealous rage, and fhamelefs thirft
   Of virtuous *Edwy*'s blood,

Had from her father's generous breaft
   Repell'd the wifh, to prove ·
An union fprung of bitter hate,
   And rough indignant love.

A letter now to meet his eye,
   The lovely maid prepares,
Which quickly to the Baron's hand
   A trufty fervant bears.

Thefe were the lines :— " From *Edbald*'s love
  " Refolv'd, at length, to fly,
" Let not the act too heinous feem
  " In a dear Father's eye.

" Nor let him judge *Edilda*'s thought
  " Unduteous e'er will prove,
" Becaufe fhe fhuns the haughty Lord,
  " Her heart could never love.

" And what but deep, yet vain remorfe,
  " What, but unceafing woe,
" From vows conftrain'd, could her fad heart,
  " Or noble *Galvan*'s know ?

" Nor has a tender Sire forgot
  " His oft-repeated vow,
" That at the altar's foot his child
  " A victim ne'er fhould bow.

" And well fhe knows his generous foul,
  " Since *Edbald*'s jealous heart
" Prompted his tongue and hand to act
  " So mean, fo bafe a part ;

" Has never wifh'd *Edilda*'s hand
  " The facrifice fhould be,
" Of pomp and pow'r, which could but glofs
  " The face of mifery.

" Then let my Lord to *Edbald*'s ear
  " His daughter's purpofe fpeak ;
" And fay, in vain his will would ftrive
  " Her firm refolve to break.

" Never from holy *Aldric*'s walls
   " *Edilda*'s feet fhall ftray,
" Till the proud Earl from *Galvan*'s court
   " For ever turn away.

" Then let him quick a fenfe of fhame
   " And fenfe of honour prove;
" Nor hang, a baleful cloud, between
   " Her and a Father's love.

" How bleft the day when once again,
   " On that dear Father's breaft,
" His child may fondly lean her head,
   " And lull his cares to reft !"

Nor was the noble maid deceiv'd;
   Nor was her Father's mind,
To favour haughty *Edbald*'s fuit,
   Still, as of late, inclin'd.

Nor did her flight difpleafure move,
   Nor letter give offence;
Since to difmifs whom now he fcorn'd,
   They offer'd fair pretence.

Full well he read the paffions foul
   That rul'd in *Edbald*'s heart;
And knew his foul had lately own'd
   A much unworthy part.

For gentle *Edwy*'s candid lines
   Had amply to his breaft
The Youth's tranfcendent honour, worth,
   And gratitude exprefs'd.

And while his cheek with tranfport glow'd,
　His heart in fecret fwore,
It valued *Edwy's* noble mind
　Each *Noble* far before.

And vow'd withal, the generous Youth
　With joy, its love fhould own,
Were but his birth one ftep above
　An abject vaffal's fon.

Alas! that pride in noble minds
　Should bear fo large a part,
And counteract the generous wifh
　And temper of the heart!

But outward circumftance, alas!
　Hath power to witch the eye,
With whom the touch of frailty leaft.
　Bewrays humanity.

Yet much the aged Warrior wail'd
　The unpropitious love,
That from his court, to want and woe,
　The gallant Shepherd drove.

And more lamented that his tongue,
　By paffion overborn,
Difmifs'd whom moft his foul approv'd,
　With fhow of pride and fcorn.

Nor yet in private did he fail
　To feek the gentle Youth,
With fair rewards, and bleffings fair,
　For all his love and truth.

K k

And of his own ungrateful heart
　Did bitterly complain,
When the preferver of himfelf
　And child was fought in vain.

For ftill its own fevereft judge,
　The generous mind appears ;
And when it errs, againft itfelf
　A dread tribunal rears.

To *Edbald* now her noble Sire
　Edilda's flight reveals ;
Nor from his heart her purpofe hides,
　Nor from his eye conceals.

But while her fcornful lines he fcann'd,
　The paffion who could fpeak
That flafh'd within his rolling eye,
　And burnt upon his cheek ?

" 'T is well ! proud maid, 'tis well !" he cry'd,
　" And *Edbald* fhall return
" Thy wretched fcorn, and foolifh pride,
　" With added pride and fcorn !

" Too highly honour'd ! wayward fair,
　" Thy heart has been by me,
" Which to a vaffal vile could ftoop
　" From all its dignity.

" Within thy paramour's bafe arms
　" Thy bafe defires enjoy ;
" Nor tremble, left my envious love
　" Thy pleafures fhould annoy."

" Now, nay, Lord *Edbald*,"—*Galvan* cry'd,
  And kindled as he faid,——
" Let not thy candour, honour, truth,
  " By paffion be betray'd.

" Nor hangs the mildew of reproach
  " Upon my Daughter's fame;
" Nor has the tongue of flander's felf
  " Dar'd fully her bright name.

" Nor canft thou, Lord, of her deceit,
  " Nor of my own complain ;
" Thou know'ft I wifh'd thy vows fuccefs,
  " And faw them fcorn'd with pain.

" And well thou know'ft thy tender cares
  " Were all too weak to move,
" Within *Edilda*'s adverfe heart,
  " The leaft return of love.

" Could *Edbald*'s vows have won her heart,
  " Thofe vows had won her hand ;
" But the refiftlefs fate of love
  " What mortal can command ?

" Yet think not fo unworthy her,
  " Nor yet fo bafe of me,
" As once to ween our fouls can ftoop
  " To one of low degree.

" Nor pitilefs arraign the Youth,
  " On whofe ill-fated head
" A hopelefs paffion all its weight
  " Of mifery hath fhed.

" Though gratitude this truth demands,
  " That had a noble birth
" His merits grac'd, the Youth had ftood
  " Unrivall'd through the earth."

" Curfe on the fpecious villain's art !"
  The haughty Lord reply'd ;
" And vain would *Galvan*'s glofing tongue
  " His fecret purpofe hide.

" Yes, abject Lord ! thy Daughter give
  " To this tranfcendent Youth,
" This pattern of intrinfic worth,
  " Of tendernefs and truth.

" But yet of noble *Edbald*'s foul
  " So little haft thou known,
" To think it tamely will give place
  " To a vile vaffal's fon ?

" No ! though I fcorn the worthlefs maid
  " Whom late my foul ador'd ;
" Though thy alliance much I fcorn,
  " Low-minded, doting Lord !

" My outrag'd honour ne'er fhall reft,
  " Till in the vital blood
" Of him I loath, this vengeful hand,
  " I fwear, be deep imbru'd !"

He fiercely faid ; and furious rufh'd
  From out the ample hall ;
Whilft much the generous *Galvan*'s heart
  His treat'nings did appal.

Not for himfelf the Noble fear'd,
　　For he ne'er ftoop'd to fear;
But for the welfare of thofe friends
　　That to his foul were dear.

But plain he kenn'd the dark revenge
　　That lowr'd in *Edbald*'s breaft;
And knew his hand would joy to act
　　The deed his tongue exprefs'd.

What, though he ween'd the gentle Youth
　　For ever paft away;
He lov'd him ftill, and wifh'd him far
　　From *Edbald*'s wrath to ftray.

Mean time, with anger in his eye,
　　And vengeance in his heart,
The haughty Earl from *Galvan*'s court
　　Indignant did depart.

To *Erpwald*'s caftle now with fpeed
　　His furious fteps advance;
From which they loiter'd had fo long,
　　Withheld by wayward chance.

Myfterious Pow'r! whofe mighty will
　　Can in one hour deftroy
The ftructure fair on which we reft
　　Our every hope of joy:

Yet o'er the foul where virtue dwells,
　　Thy reign is fhort, I truft;
And there the Phœnix Joy fhall fpring
　　More glorious! from her duft.

But curs'd the heart, where life nor death
    Her bleffings can reftore;
O! tenfold curs'd, where hope's fweet flow'r
    Withers to bloom no more!

Proud *Edbald* gone, the tidings foon
    The train to *Galvan* bear;
Nor were they, if I ween aright,
    Ungrateful to his ear.

Nor fooner did the fhades of night,
    At morn's approach decay,
Than to the well-known Abbey's gate
    The Noble hy'd away.

His prefence foon with greetings fair
    The holy *Aldric* met,
And foon with bafhful eye he view'd
    Edilda at his feet.

" Blefs me," fhe cry'd, " my honour'd Sire,
    " O blefs your child once more!"
While down her checks the trembling tears
    Of love and terror pour.

" Blefs thee, my child? O that I will,
    " While life remains," he cry'd.
And as he fpoke, the tender drops
    That dew'd her check he dry'd.

Then kindly ftooping, by the hand
    The timid maid he rais'd;
Who thus encourag'd, o'er and o'er,
    Her noble Sire embrac'd.

But who her tendernefs, her joy,
  Her gratitude, can fpeak?
Who the fweet words, that from her lips
  Of rapturous duty break,

When from her generous Father's lips
  Of *Edbald*'s flight fhe hears;
And that no more his hated love
  Shall fill her breaft with cares?

And much the friendly Abbot prais'd
  Edilda's noble foul,
That durft the mighty power of love
  At duty's call control.

And pray'd, the lenient hand of time
  Might cank'ring forrow chafe,
And frefhly tint the rofe of health
  That faded on her face.

Three peaceful days his noble guefts
  With holy *Aldric* fpend;
But on the fourth to *Galvan*'s hall
  Their journey back intend.

And now the fair adieus had paft,
  And now the outward gate
Was open'd, that the honour'd pair
  Might freely pafs thereat;

When white with foam, a courfer near,
  The company efpy'd,
On which a herald, trimly clad,
  Impetuoufly did ride.

Lo! at the Abbey's lofty gate
  He lighted is full foon,
And quick as thought at *Galvan's* feet,
  All panting, cafts him down.

Then eagerly as breath will ferve,
  His tidings doth declare;
And fhows, how *Edwy* is become
  The far-fam'd *Ofwald's* heir.

But while the wondrous tale he told,
  Th' emotions who could fpeak
That trembled in *Edilda's* eye,
  And flufh'd her Father's cheek?

With him 't was pleafure and furprife,
  Unmix'd with doubt or care;
With her 't was tranfport beating high,
  Yet dafh'd with timid fear.

Unthought-of joys his aged breaft
  With temper'd feelings move;
But her's with all the tumult throbs
  Of extafy and love.

Could Nature bear the ftrong reverfe,
  And ftill her courfe maintain?
She could not: blifs o'erftrain'd becomes
  Intolerable pain!

Thick and more thick her fighs exhale,
  Her pulfe forgets to play;
And in her Father's arms at length
  She fenfelefs funk away.

But foon from Nature's friendly paufe
   The lovely maid awakes ;
And now of bleffing's flowing cup
   More fparingly partakes :

With chaften'd joy the cordial lines
   Of noble *Ofwald* hears ;
And as fhe liftens, filent pays
   The tribute of her tears.

And fure no fweeter drops appear
   Within the melting eye,
Than thofe that fpring at joy's foft touch
   From fenfibility ?

Forthwith to noble *Galvan*'s court
   They deem it meet to hafte,
Since *Ofwald* meant to greet them there
   Before three days were pafs'd.

Yet to the Abbot, ere they go,
   Their facred word they plight,
That his blefs'd hand in Hymen's bonds
   The lovers fhall unite.

Now fpread the tidings far and near
   Of *Edwy*'s alter'd ftate ;
Nor was there one in *Galvan*'s court
   But greatly joy'd thereat.

For him they joy'd, but triumph'd more
   For fweet *Edilda*'s blifs,
Which well they ween'd, thro' life, would be
   By love involv'd in his.

And all with one confent agreed
   The charming noble pair,
Each of the other through the world
   Alone deferving were.

But who the yearnings fond could tell
   Within *Edilda's* breaft,
The hurrying thoughts, the namelefs fears,
   That pillag'd all her reft ?

As on the filent minutes ftole
   That ufher'd the glad day,
When fortune promis'd to reftore
   What duty rent away.

Yet though fhe wifh'd the feet of time
   Wing'd with the plumes of love,
And deem'd that fince the world was made
   He ne'er fo flow did move :

Still as the hour, fo wifh'd, draws nigh,
   New perturbations rife,
And chill and warm, by turns, her cheek,
   And tremble in her eyes.

And oft fhe heav'd a generous figh,
   That wealth, and pow'r, and birth,
A grace obtain'd that ftill had been
   Denied to better worth.

But if in expectation thus
   Her lovely bofom beat ;
What does it feel when fhe beholds
   Her *Edwy* at her feet!

What pen the paffions can defcribe
    That thrill within her foul?
What tongue the tranfports wild declare
    That all his pow'rs control?

Nor poor the blifs that *Galvan* taftes,
    When warmly to his breaft
The noble *Ofwald*, loft fo long,
    With love fincere he prefs'd.

Quickly the ftory of their loves
    Through all the kingdom went;
And through the land was fcarce a heart
    But fhar'd in their content.

But moft the royal *Egbert* joy'd
    The wondrous tale to hear,
For *Ofwald* joy'd, whofe wretched lot
    Had coft him many a tear.

And from his court the Monarch fent,
    With fpeed, a meffage fair,
That mickle pleafure he fhould tafte
    To greet the Lovers there.

Now focial mirth once more refounds
    Through *Galvan's* crowded hall,
And all the fmiles affembled there,
    At pleafure's grateful call.

And while the Lovers o'er and o'er
    Their tender paffion tell,
Which melting looks and ardent fighs,
    Love's language, fpoke as well;

Their aged Sires, of former times
   A thoufand tales relate,
And trace, through all her mazy rounds,
   The myftic pow'r of Fate:

Yet, now and then, amidft their talk
   Their lovely offspring view'd
With mickle pride, and faw in them
   Their blooming youth renew'd.

Where hearts were all fo well agreed,
   What need that ardent love
To Hymen long fhould fue in vain
   His happieft ftate to prove?

Soon was the nuptial torch prepar'd,
   And foon with braveft ftate
The bridal train fair iffued forth
   At *Galvan*'s lofty gate.

Ah! who that morn the rapture high
   Could paint in *Edwy*'s face?
Who the foft blufh that in the Maid's
   With tranfports blended was?

So god-like Hector fhow'd, I ween,
   When to the nuptial bed
Andromache, in beauty's bloom,
   He fweetly-bafhful led.

In trim apparel, meetly rank'd
   Upon their courfers fair,
A fplendid train, with jocund looks,
   Behind affembled were.

And ſtill, as onward flow they paſs'd,
   The country gather'd round,
And bleſs'd their ſteps, and, loving, ſtrew'd,
   With fragrant flow'rs, the ground.

On either ſide the lovely pair
   Their reverend Sires were ſeen,
Whoſe joy that morn, new grace to age,
   New fire had lent I ween.

And now to *Aldric*'s gate they came;
   And as they enter'd there,
The holy Abbot met their ſteps
   With many a welcome fair.

Quickly the Lovers graceful knelt
   Before the ſacred ſhrine;
And Hymen quick their willing hands
   With gentle bonds did join.

For virtue mated ſweet with love
   In marriage, only knows
To wear and taſte, without its thorn,
   The never-fading roſe.

At that glad hour, all words were vain
   The happineſs to tell,
Which only hearts ſo form'd as theirs
   Could merit, or could feel.

Now from the holy Abbot's gate,
   With many a bleſſing fair,
The bridal train rejoicing paſs'd
   In pageantry moſt rare!

Full in their way to *Galvan's* hall
    There ftood a pleafant grove,
Where every warbler fweetly fung
    His little tale of love:

And here, before their fteps return'd,
    Had many a youth and maid,
With fimple fhow of duteous joy,
    The boughs with garlands clad.

And while the whifpering zephyrs fent
    Their fragrance through the air,
From fultry heat the bridal train
    Was pleas'd to loiter there.

But moft the bride and bridegroom joy
    Such tokens to receive
Of humble love, and courteous fmiles,
    And praifes freely give.

Yet more to pleafe their honeft hearts
    A garland mickle fair,
The Bridegroom reach'd, and fmiling, cry'd,
    His bride the band fhould wear:

" More foft," he faid, " than this fweet wreath
    " Our gentle bands fhall prove,
" Though never, like thefe drooping flow'rs,
    " Shall fade our conftant love!"

But whilft his hand the garland gay
    Her white neck faften'd round,
A fudden cry of deep diftrefs
    Made all the grove refound.

Pale with affright *Edilda* turn'd;
   For much the fair-one fear'd
That in the cry the well-known voice
   Of her lov'd Sire she heard.

Nor judg'd amifs; for as she turn'd,
   In fwoonings she efpy'd
The aged Lord, and to his aid
   With eager duty hy'd.

But ah! alas! she little ween'd,
   Whilft, like fome timorous hind
She fped away, the heavier ill
   Her love had left behind.

For fcarce she turn'd, or e'er a shaft
   Too well directed! ftood
In *Edwy*'s breaft, and trembled there,
   And deeply drank his blood.

And fcarce its deadly point he felt,
   Or e'er the face appear'd
Of bloody *Edbald*; from whofe tongue
   This cruel taunt he heard;

" Accept, gay Bridegroom, from *this* bow
   " With joy, *that* arrow fair,
" For by thy own *Edilda*'s hand
   " They *both* prefented were !"

The finking Youth thefe bitter words
   With indignation fir'd;
While juft revenge one flafh of ftrength
   Within his breaft infpir'd.

On *Edbald* fuddenly he rufh'd,
   As bafe he turn'd his head
To fly the grove; and by the reins
   Reftrain'd his fiery fteed.

Then cried, as high he rais'd his hand,
   " Remember, treacherous Lord!
" That when to *thee* fhe gave a bow,
   " To *me* fhe gave a fword."

He faid; and in the villain's breaft
   Plung'd deep the fhining blade,
Which found the paffage to his heart,
   And mix'd him with the dead.

But little to the noble Youth
   Avails his vengeance juft;
Ah! what avails his haughty foe
   Stretch'd filent in the duft;

Since faft life's purple current ebbs,
   And yet once more he tries
To feek his fweet *Edilda's* face,
   But as he looks he dies.

Loud, and more loud, *Edilda's* fhrieks
   Re-echoed through the grove,
While to her *Edwy* faft fhe flew,
   By terror borne and love.

Alas! 't was dread of this diftrefs
   That riv'd her Father's heart,
As fudden through the fhade he faw
   Bafe *Edbald* aim the dart.

Nor knew the Bride the work of fate,
  Till to his hall with care
Her Sire, in deadly fwoonings laid,
  She bade the fervants bear.

But feeking then whom moft fhe lov'd,
  Whom moft fhe lov'd fhe fpy'd ;
Yet ere her eyes that fight beheld
  Had rather far have dy'd.

Ah! who could think her *Edwy*'s face
  An object e'er would be,
In her fond eye, of horror wild,
  And deepeft mifery ?

But not alone at *Edwy*'s fate
  Her bitter forrows flow ;
Nor fhe alone muft claim the fad
  Prerogative of woe :

Age joins with Youth at fuch a fcene,
  To wage a cruel war
With grief, whofe all-relentlefs hand
  Points firmly to defpair.

And who can marvel that a heart
  Awak'd from length of woe
To fudden joy, at woe's return
  A deep defpair fhould know ?

O! he that *can*, has never fure,
  Like wretched *Ofwald*, known
The lofs of all his hopes on earth
  In lofing fuch a Son !

O o

To *Edwy*'s corfe, with burfting heart,
  The haplefs Noble fped;
And wrung his hands in fpeechlefs woe,
  And fhook his hoary head.

Forthwith on either fide the corfe
  With many a bitter groan,
The childlefs Sire, and widow'd Bride,
  Diftracted throw them down.

A thoufand and a thoufand times
  The body they embrace;
A thoufand and a thoufand times
  They kifs the pallid face.

A thoufand and a thoufand times
  To fpeak, in vain they try;
Upon their wan and quiv'ring lips
  The murmuring accents die.

But when within her *Edwy*'s breaft
  Edilda fcann'd the dart;
She frantic cry'd, " Almighty Pow'rs!
  " This hand has pierc'd his heart!

" O yes, his own *Edilda*'s hand
  " The fatal fhaft fupply'd;
" By which, far dearer than her life,
  " Her lovely Hufband dy'd!"

She faid; and recklefs what to do,
  Or where to find relief,
On *Ofwald*'s bofom, o'er the corfe
  Reclin'd, and hid her grief.

Ah! then the piteous fight to fee,
  His reverend filver hairs
Hang o'er *Edilda*'s faded cheek,
  And drink her falling tears.

Around the late-gay bridal train
  With folemn filence wait,
And weep alike the Mourner's woe,
  And gallant *Edwy*'s fate.

Still o'er the breathlefs, bleeding youth
  The wretched Mourners bend,
While on the wan, yet lovely face,
  Their ftreaming forrows blend:

Still did they bend, ftill did they weep,
  When with an angel's fpeed,
A learned Leech, from *Galvan*'s hall,
  Flew in that hour of need.

And though on *Edwy*'s pallid face
  He ftrove in vain to feek
The life-warm blood that us'd to ftain
  With vermeil hue his cheek ;

Though on his wan, *wan* lips in vain
  He fought the ruby pride,
With which the foft and fwelling twins
  Erewhile were doubly dy'd ;

Yet in his *pulfe*, at fearful paufe,
  Fond life yet, lingering, beat ;
And in his bofom yet was felt
  Its laft retiring heat.

" Be comforted ! for ftill he lives,"
 The Sage, exulting, cry'd ;
" O ! blefling, blefling on that tongue !"
 The trembling Fair reply'd.

" O ! blefling, blefling on that tongue !"
 Exclaim'd the hoary Sire,
" Which lights, once more, within my breaft,
 " Sweet hope's extinguifh'd fire.

A fovereign cordial now apply'd,
 Life's dying flame revives ;
Though ftill, but by convulfive ftarts,
 The noble *Edwy* lives.

O ! what was reverend *Ofwald*'s joy
 No language can reveal,
As o'er his *Edwy*'s check once more
 He faw the crimfon fteal.

No tongue can tell the joy that rufh'd
 Upon *Edilda*'s foul,
As o'er her lover's lips again
 The warm carnation ftole !

To *Galvan*'s court, with cautious ftep,
 The gallant Youth was mov'd,
And watch'd with fond inceffant care
 By every eye he lov'd.

Around his couch, with filent foot,
 Each anxious Parent crept,
And o'er him long, his peerlefs Bride
 Alternate fmil'd and wept.

For long, 'twixt life and death, the Youth
    With frequent fwoonings lay;
Till by the power of foft'ning balms
    The fhaft was drawn away.

From that bleft hour with freer pulfe
    Life beat within his breaft,
And riper rofes on his cheek,
    Returning health confeft.

O! from his bright expreffive eye
    When now fhe glitter'd fair,
How did his fweet indignant Bride
    The hated arrow tear!

On every eddy of the wind
    A feveral wreck was borne,
And all its filver pride defac'd,
    With mingled rage and fcorn.

And oft, with fervour, on his breaft,
    She, trembling, kifs'd the fcar,
And, like the dew-drop on the thorn,
    Adorn'd it with a tear.

Long bleft, and bleffing all around,
    Uncloying, and uncloy'd,
They liv'd; and long their happinefs
    Their noble Sires enjoy'd.

Long did their numerous offspring live,
    Their country's boaft, and pride,
And ftill *fhall* live, while love, and truth,
    And honour, fhall abide:

For every brave and generous youth
   Shall *Edwy*'s praifes fhare,
And emulate, ye Britifh maids,
   That fhining morning ftar.

A morning ftar *Edilda* fhines,
   Your wandering fteps to guide,
That ye may trace life's wildering maze,
   With honour's nobleft pride.

As the coy violet lifts its head
   Amid the vernal fnows,
And, breathing lavifh fragrance round,
   With purple beauty glows;

So may their honour'd memories live,
   As frefh as in their prime,
And blufh, and breathe their fragrance round
   Upon the fnows of time!

Ah! happy, whofoe'er extracts
   The honey from fuch flow'rs,
And with perennial fweetnefs decks
   Life's tranfitory hours.

THE END.